DIADEM

D1114313

Look for the other books in the

#1 Book of Names

#2 Book of Signs

#3 Book of Magic

Coming soon:

#5 Book of Earth

#6 Book of Nightmares

Book of Thunder

John Peel

SCHOLASTIC INC.
New York Toronto London Auckland Sydney

ISBN 0-590-05950-5

12 11 10 9 8 7 6 5 4 3 2 7 8 9/9 0 1 2/0

Printed in the U.S.A.
First Scholastic printing, October 1997

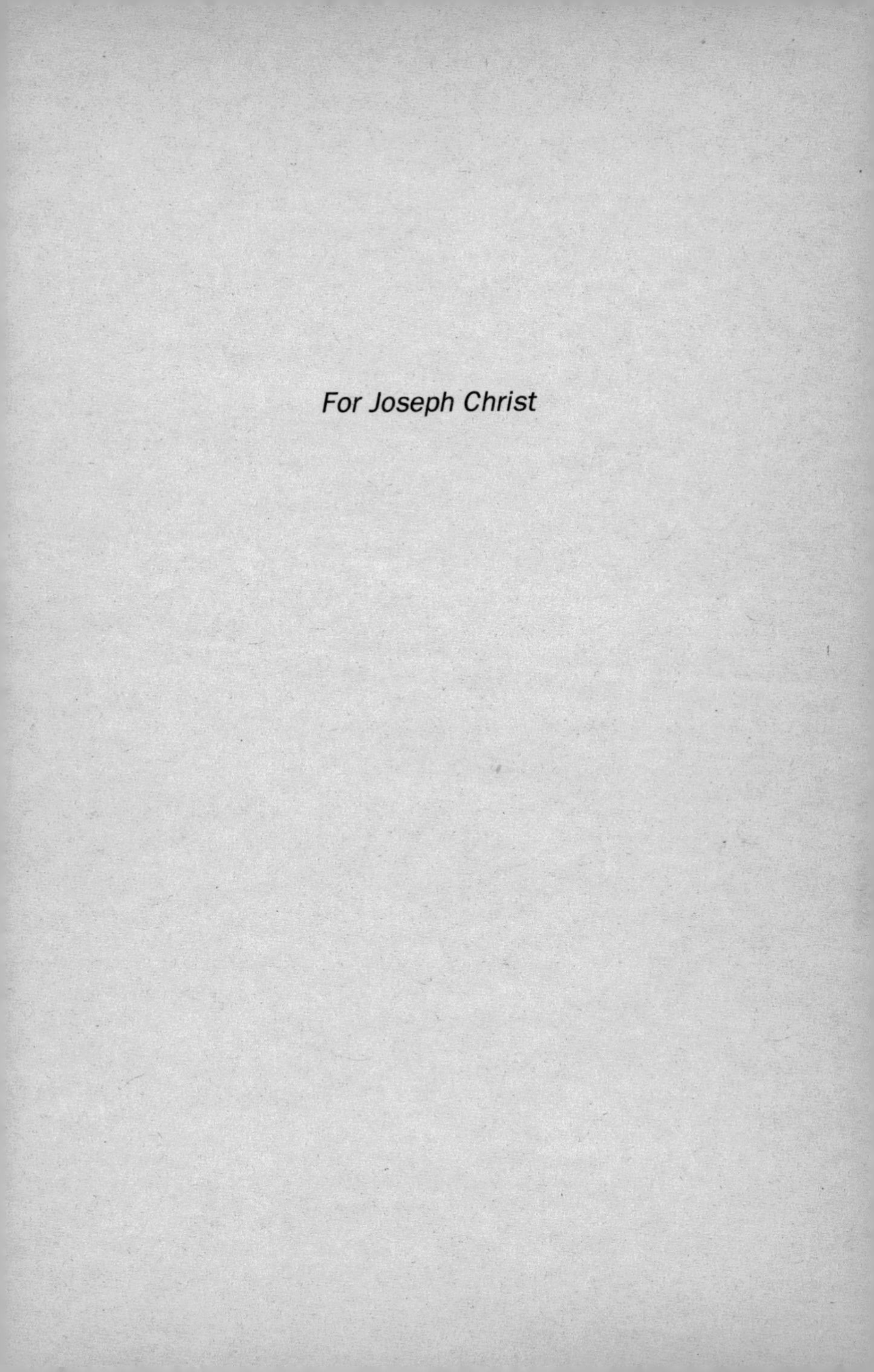

For Joseph Christ

DIADEM

PROLOGUE

"You again!" Shanara snapped, looking up from her work. "What do you want?"

The intruder in the wizard's study smiled cheerily back at her. "So nice to see you, too, Shanara," Oracle murmured politely. "How's Blink?" he added, referring to the wizard's familiar, a red panda.

"Sleeping, as usual," Shanara answered. "Now, what do you want?" Her eyes narrowed. "And how is it that you're no longer speaking in that irritating poetic style of yours?"

"I can always return to it, if you wish," Oracle answered. He brushed imaginary dirt off his jet-black clothing; considering the fact that he didn't really exist in this dimension, and was merely a projection, it was impossible that he should have any real dust on him. "But I've been cured. I'm enjoying my newfound liberty to say what I like when I like."

Shanara sighed and closed the book she'd been studying. "If you're here to speak, then speak. Otherwise, go back to your masters and let me alone."

Oracle inclined his head slightly. "I bring you news," he informed her. "My former masters are no more. Added to that, Sarman and his Shadows have been vanquished, and all's right with the Diadem."

The wizard's eyebrows rose, and she finally smiled. "Really?" she exclaimed happily. "And my three friends? Score, Pixel, and Helaine?"

"Came through," confirmed Oracle. "They won the great battle, and they're now back on Dondar. I thought you might like to know, since you seemed to be quite fond of them."

"They're good kids," Shanara answered. "I'm glad they're safe."

Oracle frowned slightly. "I didn't say they were *safe*," he replied. "On the contrary, they have an astonishing knack for getting into trouble."

"Do they need my help?" asked Shanara quickly. It was obvious that she was concerned for them.

Oracle shrugged. "It's hard to say. But there's nothing you can do for them anyway. Dondar is on the

Inner Circuit. If you attempt to travel there, you know the magical overload would kill you."

She glared at him. "So you came all this way just to make me worry about them? Thanks a lot."

"I have great confidence in them," Oracle replied haughtily. "They defeated Sarman and the Triad, and came up with an elegant solution to the problem of misbehaving magic. I'm sure that they'll be able to overcome what faces them now." Then he looked concerned. "Of course, I can't be sure exactly what it is they face yet, so I may be wrong. All I know is that they've made friends with one of the unicorn herds on Dondar, and their friends are in grave danger."

"Unicorns?" Shanara looked wistful. "I always wanted to meet one. And they've made friends with a whole *herd*? That sounds like the three of them, all right." She stared at him. "Can't you go to them and help them?"

"Go to them, yes," Oracle answered. "Help them? No. I don't know what it is they're facing." He gave her a significant look. "On the other hand, if you were to wake up that lazy Blink, maybe the two of you might be able to discover some nugget of information that I could take to Score, Helaine, and Pixel. It might just save their lives."

"Right." Shanara was suddenly all business.

"Blink!" she yelled loudly. "Get out of bed and get to work."

"Work?" a sleepy voice asked indignantly. A reddish face with black markings appeared out of a deep pile of cushions. "You know I *hate* that word."

"And I know you love the word *food*," Shanara snapped back. "And if you want any of the latter, you'd better do some of the former."

Blink sighed, yawned, and then stretched. "It's a rough life," he complained.

"We all have to make sacrifices," Oracle said, unsympathetically. "I just hope that Helaine, Pixel, and Score don't end up sacrificing their lives before we can help them."

CHAPTER 1

Score was amazed at how easily they had created their first gateway, taking them from Jewel to Dondar. It gave him quite a rush to realize that he and his friends had become quite adept at this magic business. Of course, they still had an immense amount to learn, and they had lost some of their power back on Jewel. But, still, this whole thing was astonishing.

Barely a week ago, he'd been a lost, frightened kid living on the streets of New York City. Now he was a magic-user, one of the strongest in all of the worlds that made up the Diadem. And he was no longer alone — he now had friends.

There was Helaine. He'd first gotten to know her in her disguise as the boy Renald. She'd been arrogant, aggressive, and cold then. Now she seemed to have changed a whole lot. She was smiling with ease, and she'd bonded with Score after the adventures they went through together. She was an incredible fighter, and didn't seem to know what fear was.

And there was Pixel. The other boy had grown up in a world of Virtual Reality, which he'd given up when he wanted something *real*. He wasn't really very good at coping with practical, everyday life. But he'd proven he was braver than he looked, and incredibly bright. He could make sense out of extremely cryptic information.

All in all, Score couldn't think of two people he'd rather have as friends, and he was glad that they felt the same way about him, despite his failings. Score was very honest with himself about those. He'd grown up on the streets, terrified of his father and of the dangers all around him. His instinct had always been to run away from trouble. He'd never been able to trust anyone for fear of being turned on. So he had problems relating to other people. Helaine and Pixel knew this, and made allowances. Score supposed that was what friendship was all about. He'd never known it before.

Moving through the Diadem, they had survived several threats to their lives. After defeating the evil wizard Sarman, they had been looking forward to a rest. But then Helaine had picked up a distress call from Flame. They knew they had to return to the world of Dondar immediately.

To do this, they had created a gateway between worlds. As they stepped out of the jagged tear in space, Score saw that they were back in the castle that had once belonged to the dark wizard Garonath. He had tried to kill the three of them, but had been defeated by Thunder and several of his fellow unicorns. Unicorn horns could negate magic, and they had cut Garonath off from his power — causing him to wither into dust, as he'd prolonged his life artificially by use of his magic. Since he had left no heirs, Score figured that his castle and everything in it belonged to him, Pixel, and Helaine now. It needed a bit of work, but it might one day become kind of a pleasant place to live. "This Old Castle," thought Score, grinning.

But right now, there was the cry for help to handle.

Flame was waiting for them in the courtyard, tapping her forehoof impatiently. She was a beautiful creature, white, with flecks of pure gold in her skin. Her long, spiral horn glittered in the torchlight of the room. She tossed her head and thought at them: *At last! Thank goodness you're all safe!*

"What's wrong?" asked Helaine, moving forward to stroke her friend. She and Flame had bonded; it was part of the reason why Helaine had loosened up. You couldn't love a unicorn and be a grouch.

It's my father, explained Flame. *He's facing the Rite of Combat.*

Score scowled. Thunder could be a real problem sometimes. He was suspicious and opinionated. But he was fair, and brave, and Score rather liked him. Not that he got all mushy over Thunder, as Helaine did with Flame. It was just respect, that was all. He wasn't going to get worked up about a horse with a horn. Still, he didn't like the sound of what Flame had just thought. It felt weird, talking to a unicorn and then hearing her reply inside his head. But Score was getting used to it.

"Rite of Combat?" he asked. "What's that?"

Flame tossed her head. *Can we talk about it on the way?* she asked. *It might begin anytime now, and I'm really afraid my father might need some help.*

"Let's go," agreed Pixel. Score and Helaine nodded, so Flame whirled around and led the way. She was clearly impatient to be off and running, but she knew that none of the humans could keep up with her if she did. The castle of Garonath was built on the edge of the unicorns' pastures. One of Thunder's jobs as leader of his herd was to keep their pastures free of any intruders and other problems. Garonath had wisely stayed out of his way, until he'd gotten too greedy for unicorn horns.

As you know, explained Flame, *each unicorn herd is led by a single, dominant leader. His job is to guard and protect the herd from any dangers, so he has to be the strongest and best in the herd. The way that this is ensured is that any unicorn is allowed to challenge the leader to combat for the position. If the leader wins, the challenger must leave the herd. Sometimes they become wanderers, and other times they try challenging a less powerful leader of another herd for the position. If the challenger wins, the old leader is either killed or banished.*

"It sounds a bit rough to me," Score complained. "Couldn't they just draw straws for it, or something?"

Helaine gave him a dark look. "It's an honorable practice that is also known on my world," she said. "It ensures that only the strongest and best will lead." She turned back to Flame. "Your father is a noble person," she said comfortingly. "Surely he'll be able to take on this challenger without much of a problem?"

Normally, I'd agree with you, replied Flame. *But my father has never faced the Rite of Combat before.*

"Huh?" asked Pixel. "Then how did he become leader? You just said that this was how it always happened."

*How it's *supposed* to happen,* corrected Flame.

*But the old leader of our herd was Darkstar. Thunder loved him, and would never have challenged him for control of the herd. You see, just because you *can* make a challenge doesn't mean you *have* to. None of our herd would ever challenge Thunder, either.*

"I'm definitely not understanding all of this," Score complained. They had reached the boundaries of the unicorn lands now, and the going was easy. There were all sorts of trails through it that the herd kept clear.

Darkstar was never defeated for control of the herd, Flame explained. *He simply vanished one day and was never seen again. Since Thunder was Darkstar's favorite, everyone simply accepted him as the new leader. He's very popular you know.* She sounded very proud of her father.

"We know," agreed Helaine. "But you said that nobody in the herd would ever challenge your father. So what's this Rite of Combat challenge?"

It's an outsider, Flame answered. *A rogue male named Tychus. He must have left some other herd, and now he's decided to challenge my father for control of our herd.*

"Oh." Score shrugged. "Surely Thunder can defeat him." Flame didn't answer. "Well, *can't* he?"

Maybe, Flame finally agreed. She sounded anything but certain. *But I've seen Tychus. He's a lot bigger than my father, and he seems to have . . . I don't know. There's an air of *wrongness* about him. But the laws of our people say that once a challenge has been issued, it must be met. My father has to go through with this.* She gave a mental sigh. *And there's another problem, too. My father thinks that the old code of Rite of Combat is barbaric and should have been stopped centuries ago. His heart isn't in the fight.*

"If you ask me, your father's right," Score replied. "All this macho fighting stuff is junk. So do you want us to stop the fight?"

No! exclaimed Flame, appalled. *That is forbidden. No one is allowed to stop a Rite. Once a challenge has been given, it must be met.*

"Sounds dumb to me," admitted Score. "Can't Thunder just abdicate, or something?"

Abdicate? Flame sounded shocked. *My father would never back away from a challenge.*

"Then he's a fool," Score said.

"It's a matter of honor," explained Helaine.

"Well, that's why I don't get it, then," Score answered with a grin. "I don't have any honor, so I can't see any point in fighting over it."

Besides, added Flame, exasperated, *my father takes his task as herd leader very seriously. He wouldn't just leave them when they still needed him.*

"I'm getting some of the picture here," Pixel said. He was starting to get a little winded from running. He still wasn't too used to exercise, and was finding reality a lot harder to cope with sometimes than he'd ever expected. Still, he was managing pretty well. "But if Thunder's going through with it anyway, what do you expect us to do?"

There was a short pause, and then Flame shook her head. *I don't really know,* she admitted. *But I'm *scared*. I wanted the three of you by us. I thought that since you're Thunder's friends, you'd want to be present.*

"We do," agreed Helaine. "But we're strictly not allowed to intervene?"

It's absolutely forbidden, Flame answered, miserably. *Otherwise I'd ask you to do some magic to set everything right.*

"This sounds like one case where magic won't help out," Helaine said grimly. "But we'll do what we can."

"And we'll definitely be cheering Thunder on," agreed Score. He was starting to get tired himself. "Look, do we have much farther to go?"

No, said Flame, to his immense relief. *The combat ground is by the river just ahead.*

Score could see the trees thinning out there. His eyes widened as he saw the shapes by the combat ground. Though he, Helaine, and Pixel had heard of Thunder's herd, they had never actually seen it.

There had to be over a hundred unicorns here, in all shades and hues. Not just horse colors, like white, brown, and black. There were oranges, purples, blues, and violets, tinged with silver, gold, copper, and scarlet. It was an astonishing array of colors, all topped by flashing horns.

The unicorns parted to let them through. Score could feel dozens of eyes on him. Most of the unicorns, he knew, had never seen a human before. Most humans couldn't get this far into the Diadem. Only magic-users could do that. And few of them made it. Those few that did tended to be selfish, arrogant, and aloof — and most of the rest were nasty and lethal. The unicorn policy, pretty wisely, had been to avoid humans at all cost.

Score, Helaine, and Pixel were the first exceptions this herd had ever made to that policy. Several of the foals stared at the humans in astonishment and a little fear. Score grinned back at them, resisting the temptation to yell "Boo!" A couple of the more nervous ones ran to hide behind their mothers.

At the edge of the river, a large space had been cleared. There were no trees, shrubs, or rocks here. It was like a large football field, level and virtually bare. This was obviously the combat zone. By the edge of the water, Thunder and his wife, Nova, were waiting, their tails flicking impatiently.

Thunder was a large creature, and very impressive. His hide was deep black, with splashes of white in the coat like stars. Nova was a cheerful reddish-pink, with blotches of purple in that. She was smaller than her husband, but no less impressive.

So, Thunder thought at them, *you've come to watch the fight? Typical humans, with a love of violence.*

"Hey, this wasn't our idea," Score snapped back. "You're the one being violent, not us. We came here to cheer you on. Or," he added with a wicked grin, "maybe we should be rooting for the challenger. He might be a little less grouchy than you."

You are welcome to be here, Nova thought at them, preventing her husband from responding. *You are aware that you must not interfere in any way?*

"Yes," Pixel assured her. "But we had to be here as a show of support."

Thank you, she replied graciously. Then she glanced around. *Well, it seems as though the only thing missing now is Tychus, the challenger.*

"Maybe he's chickened out?" suggested Score hopefully.

One of the other unicorns moved forward, nervously. *Thunder,* he said. *We do not allow humans among us. You yourself have often said that they cannot be trusted.*

Ah . . . er, yes, that's true, agreed Thunder. *But . . .*

Score enjoyed watching him be so embarrassed.

*These humans *can* be trusted,* Thunder finally said. *And they will take an oath to help and not harm the herd, won't you?*

We certainly will, agreed Score, and his friends echoed him. *I promise that I will never cause harm to come to this herd, and that I shall be friends with it always.*

Nicely put, Pixel said, approvingly. He and Helaine echoed the same words.

Right, Thunder announced. *That promise having been given, I think everyone should agree that they can visit us when they like in friendship.* The entire herd echoed his words. Thunder then turned back to the humans and added, gruffly: *All right, you're accepted. Just behave yourselves, understand?*

There was a sudden movement at the edge of the crowd, and the unicorns there began parting.

"No such luck," muttered Pixel gloomily. "Look."

A large unicorn made his way imperiously through the throng. He was almost pure red, with flecks of white throughout his coat. He held his head arrogantly high.

Score couldn't suppress a shiver. He could see why Flame had been worried. Thunder was large and muscular, but this newcomer was even larger, by almost six inches. His muscles rippled beneath his coat as he made his self-assured way through the watchers.

Thunder! Even his mental greeting was a cry of challenge. If it had been audible, it would have been loud enough to be painful. As it was, Score winced as it seemed to echo through his head. *Enough delays! Now let the combat begin!*

Lowering his head, Tychus pawed the ground and then charged forward, his horn poised to skewer Thunder where he stood.

CHAPTER 2

Helaine gasped at the sudden violent action. She, Score, and Pixel jumped back out of the path of Tychus's charge. Flame gasped and did likewise.

Thunder whirled around, snorting furiously, and jumped to the side. Tychus, unable to stop his charge in time, shot past Thunder. The black unicorn smacked his horn across Tychus's rear as he flashed by. It was more humiliating than painful, and Helaine could hear a mental ripple of laughter from the assembled unicorns.

"I *knew* Thunder could take him," Score said proudly.

“That was just the first move,” Helaine replied. “Let’s see what happens now.”

Nova had also moved back, joining her daughter at the edge of the crowd. Thunder and Tychus now had a large, clear area for their battle. Tychus ground to a halt, dust fluttering about his hooves. He turned back to face Thunder, who was waiting patiently.

A lucky move, Tychus growled.

Perhaps, Thunder answered mockingly. *More likely a foolish move on your part.* He whinnied and added: *I’m ready when you are.*

Tychus snorted, pawed at the ground, and then charged again. Helaine could see that he was ready for Thunder to skip aside again, and was running a little more slowly so he could twist to the attack at the last moment. But Thunder had no intention of repeating the same tactic twice. Instead, he, too, leaped forward, running hard and fast at his opponent.

There was a loud *crack!* as they met halfway across the field. Helaine gasped in fear, thinking that both horns must have shattered under the force of the blow. To her amazement, both unicorns appeared intact, and merely dazed by the force with which they had struck one another.

The blows were taken on the forehead, not the horns, Flame informed her. *It’s like two humans butting heads — painful, but endurable.*

Maybe so, thought Helaine, but it wasn't a tactic she'd like to use.

Shaking his head to clear it, Thunder stepped back. He was refusing to attack Tychus, leaving his opponent to instigate battle again. Helaine could understand this: Thunder had no real desire for the fight, and he was hoping that Tychus would call it off. But Helaine could see by the ferocious flash of Tychus's eyes that he had no intention of stopping until one of the combatants was dead. Helaine thought Thunder was being very foolish. He should start to attack, not just defend himself.

Tychus snorted loudly and reared up on his hind legs, striking out at Thunder with his forefeet. Thunder responded in kind, rearing up and kicking out. For a minute, they danced around on their hind legs, thrusting at each other. Both were breathing heavily, but neither was making any headway. Despite their difference in size, they were pretty evenly matched.

Then Tychus fell back to all fours and stepped away from Thunder. Thunder allowed himself to settle down, warily watching for the next move from his challenger. Tychus lowered his head slightly, though not enough to use his horn, and charged Thunder. Again, Thunder met him halfway. This time, the impact was taken by their sides as they slammed into each other and rebounded. Tychus immediately hurled himself against Thunder again, ramming him one more time. Thunder staggered back slightly, shook his head, and then charged in himself. This time it was Tychus who reeled back, winded.

"Go for him, Thunder!" Helaine yelled. "Don't wait for the attack."

But he either didn't hear her or else he paid her no attention. Once more, Thunder waited for Tychus to restart the fight. Both unicorns were panting now, clouds of hot, moist breath about their muzzles. Tychus backed off, put his head down, and charged.

Thunder skipped to one side again, but Tychus had been expecting this. He whirled his head about, trying to gouge Thunder's side with his horn as he passed. Thunder had been expecting *that*, though, and his own horn intercepted Tychus's. There was another loud crack, and sparks flew as the horns met, parried, and slid apart.

Thunder was doing well so far, but Helaine was still worried. By refusing to attack while his foe was turning, Thunder was giving Tychus the chance to recover his breath and prepare another attack. It was all very noble of Thunder, but terribly foolish. Helaine knew that when fighting a foe like this, the best thing to do was to end the fight quickly. Tychus was larger, and would have more stamina. It was quite possible that he would wear down Thunder in the long run.

This time, Tychus came back and reared up, lunging out with his hooves again. Thunder countered this, and for several moments it was like watching a boxing match between the two unicorns. Each lashed out with their forehooves, trying to score a blow, and trying to intercept the blows struck against them.

Thunder's hoof connected with Tychus's chest. The hard hoof left a trail of bright blood across the unicorn's hide. Tychus grunted in pain and pulled back a moment.

"First blood to Thunder!" yelled Score happily. "Way to go!"

"It's not over yet," cautioned Helaine.

"Ah, don't be such a downer," Score said. "Thunder's going to beat this idiot." He grinned as he used Thunder's favorite phrase: "You mark my words!"

Helaine hoped that Score was right, but she wasn't so sure. Flame had mentioned earlier that there seemed to be something wrong about Tychus, and Helaine could feel it, too. She'd been in enough fights in her time to realize that Tychus held something in reserve. But what? He clearly had some sort of a plan, and Thunder wasn't apparently aware of this fact. Despite having the advantage, Thunder was just standing there, panting and waiting for Tychus to start again.

Which Tychus did. The slash across his chest was probably burning, but it wasn't severe enough to slow or stop him. With the frenzy of the fight, Tychus would hardly feel it. As he drew close to Thunder, his horn came down again.

This time, Thunder stood his ground, lowering his own head only at the last moment. His horn was under Tychus's, so when Thunder threw up his head, it forced Tychus's horn and head upward. Their cheeks collided, and Thunder pushed sideways, sending Tychus reeling away.

But Thunder had taken quite a blow, and his head had to be ringing from it. He seemed dazed, and Tychus noticed it. He wasn't as gallant as Thunder, and had no problem with attacking an unprepared foe. With a snort, he threw himself back at Thunder, his horn down for a strike.

At the last second, Thunder skipped aside again, and Helaine let her breath out in a rush of relief. Thunder had been faking! As Tychus missed him, Thunder's horn scored a quick blow against the red stallion's flank. Tychus neighed in pain, and whirled to face Thunder again. Specks of blood splashed from the cut across his flank.

Tychus seemed to have lost all control now. He tried kicking, head-butting, and simply ramming himself against Thunder. Thunder managed to counter each attack, but was falling slowly back toward the river under the repeated impacts. Helaine couldn't help worrying, because Thunder seemed to be tiring faster that his opponent.

Then Tychus got past Thunder's guard. His horn flashed, and struck. It impacted in a long, shallow cut down the side of Thunder's neck, leaving bright blood flowing from the wound. At the same time, though, Thunder's horn scored down Tychus's side.

Both unicorns danced back, blood dripping from their own bodies, onto their mother-of-pearl horns.

Thunder stumbled slightly, almost giddily.

With a roar, Tychus threw himself forward, slamming his body against Thunder's. Helaine winced at the force of the blow. Thunder staggered and almost fell. He was shaking his head as if trying to clear it. Was this another trick to lure Tychus in close? Helaine's eyes narrowed as she watched.

Tychus reared up and kicked out with his hooves. Thunder didn't even try to defend himself. One foot slammed into his ribs, the other into his neck. Thunder wheezed, staggering aside. Then he fell to his knee on the left front leg, shaking his head continually.

Radiating triumph, Tychus slammed his body against Thunder again. This time, Thunder grunted in pain and fell to his side, panting and gasping. He tried to raise his head and pawed ineffectually at the ground with his hooves, trying to rise again and face his foe.

Helaine couldn't understand what was happening. She was certain that Thunder hadn't been hurt that badly; why was he having so much trouble, then?

Thunder was still struggling ineffectually to rise. Tychus lowered his horn and moved in for the kill.

Shocked, Helaine realized that even though Tychus had won the fight quite clearly, he was still intending to kill Thunder as he lay there helplessly. Technically, it was within his rights as victor, she knew, but practically, it was no better than murder.

As Tychus started to charge toward the fallen Thunder, Score gave a low growl and stepped forward. "No!" he exclaimed, and then muttered under his breath. Helaine had a very good idea of what he was doing.

A wall of fire immediately sprang up between Thunder and Tychus, and the crimson unicorn had to swerve aside to avoid being burned. He shook his head and ground to a halt. Finally he turned to stare at Score, who was standing in front of the assembled crowd, his arms folded across his chest.

*You *interfered*, boy,* the unicorn thought at him, darkly. *No one is allowed to interfere in a Rite of Combat.*

"Stuff it," Score replied. Helaine discovered that she was very proud of him. He was actually acting bravely to save the life of his friend. Wonders would never cease! Score gave a nasty little grin. "I'm changing the rules, here and now. And if you or anyone else —" He glared at the other assembled unicorns, daring them to think anything "— don't like it, then you'll have to deal with me."

"And me," Helaine said immediately, stepping forward to join him.

"Ditto," added Pixel, on the other side of Score.

Nova gave a nervous whinny. *This is not allowed,* she exclaimed. *Tychus has the right to finish the fight. It is our law.*

"It's not just some silly rule we're talking about here," Pixel said. "It's your husband's *life.* Do you *want* him to die?"

No! Nova exclaimed. *Of course not! But it is the law.*

"Not anymore," Score said, refusing to back down. "We're changing that law. Tychus has won; that should be enough for him. If it isn't, he can fight us." He gave Helaine and Pixel a thankful smile, and took his chrysolite out of his pocket. "As a magician, I have *very* strong powers. Watch." He held up the gemstone, and focused his thoughts. Chrysolite gave him the power over the element of Water. He concentrated and a section of the river froze over, despite the heat of the day. Then he glared at Tychus. "The blood in your body is mostly water," he said. "How'd you like me to turn all of *that* into ice?"

Tychus stood hesitantly where he was, eyeing Score with a good deal of respect and worry. Then he tossed his head, his mane and horn sparkling in the sunlight. *The boy is right!* he proclaimed telepathically. *I have defeated Thunder and have proven that I am now worthy to lead the herd in his place. Let the fallen one live. It is of no concern to me.*

"Smart move," muttered Score. Helaine knew that he'd never admit it, but he had been very concerned for Thunder. Though the two of them constantly argued, they were both very fond of one another.

"Well done," Helaine told him approvingly. "I'm amazed at how brave you're getting."

"Brave?" Score gave a nervous laugh. "I was shaking in my sneakers, I was so scared. I'm not brave."

"Yes you are," she insisted. "Anyone can act bravely if they don't know fear. It takes a truly brave person to face their fears and refuse to give in to them. I'm proud of you."

"Really?" He gave her a very odd look. "Nobody's ever been proud of me before."

Helaine laughed. "Then I guess we're all learning to change."

"We'd better see how Thunder is," Pixel commented.

"Right." Score used the chrysolite to shower water from the river onto the fire he had started. When it was out, the three of them moved forward. Nova and Flame ran on ahead, both very concerned.

Tychus strode forward. *I have won,* he announced. *I expect all of you now to pledge your loyalty to me.* He stared at the closest unicorns. *Beginning immediately.*

One by one, the unicorns began to move forward. Each of them knelt before the triumphant Tychus, and went to their knees on their forelegs. *I pledge my service and loyalty only to Tychus,* each of them said.

Helaine felt sickened by this, but she knew that the unicorns had no choice in the matter. By their own laws, they had to do this. Still, only a short while ago they had been loyal to Thunder. Many of them, she knew, would not have taken the oath if they had any way of avoiding it.

"How is he?" Score asked, bending over Thunder. Both Nova and Flame were nuzzling him, examining his wounds.

Helaine looked herself. One of the things she'd been trained to do as a warrior on her home world of

Ordin was to look after her warhorse. This was an important part of a soldier's duty, because a good warhorse was more valuable than an average soldier, and harder to come by. Unicorns weren't the same as horses, of course, but they were similar. She frowned as she studied Thunder's wounds. There were the two gashes, neither of them terribly severe, and the start of a large bruise on his side where he had collided with Tychus. But that appeared to be all. It was definitely not enough for him to be in this state. It simply didn't make sense.

He's incoherent, Nova answered. *His mind's a jumble. He can't think straight.*

"Perhaps when he and Tychus bashed heads he got a concussion?" suggested Pixel.

"It's a thought," Helaine agreed. She knelt beside the wheezing Thunder and gently felt his forehead and the base of his horn. "There's no sign of a fracture or other damage," she announced. "There doesn't seem to be any damage. His skull's very thick."

"You're telling me," said Score, but there was none of his usual bite in the insult. He was too worried. "So why's he gone like this?"

I don't know, admitted Nova. *He must be more badly hurt than we thought.* She sounded very concerned and scared for her husband.

"Can we move him?" asked Pixel. "I mean, I don't know much about unicorns at all, but maybe we need to wrap him up and keep him warm. And he could probably do with some medication for those cuts, before they get infected."

I think we'd be better leaving him here, Nova answered. *At least, until he gets a little better.*

Tychus pushed his way forward, glaring down at them all. *He cannot stay here,* he announced. *He has been defeated. I have spared his life, but he can no longer live on herd grounds. He must leave immediately. If he is still on herd grounds at sunset, wizards or no wizards, I promise you that I shall kill him.* He stared at Helaine, then at Pixel, and then finally at Score. *The rest of the herd has sworn allegiance to me, now. If I order them, they must kill Thunder — and anyone who stands in their way. Perhaps you can stop one unicorn with your magics, humans. But can you stop us all?*

Helaine felt sick to her stomach. She knew that if she had to, she could bring herself to injure or even kill Tychus for the sake of Thunder. But the others? She looked around the herd. They didn't want to obey such an order, she knew, but they would be forced to do so if Tychus demanded it. Unicorns were very honorable creatures and they had pledged him their loyalty.

Even if she thought they could win, Helaine didn't want to hurt the herd at all. Tychus knew that, and knew that he had won.

"If we move him, he may die," argued Score.

If you do not move him, he will certainly die, promised Tychus. *You must take him away from here, and he must never return.*

Helaine didn't know what to do next. She stared at Thunder, and could feel tears forming in her eyes.

CHAPTER 3

Pixel realized that he really hated Tychus. The crimson unicorn was being deliberately nasty. Tychus hoped that moving Thunder would kill him, clearly, and save him the trouble. There had to be something that they could do to save the situation, but what? The only advantage they had was magic.

Maybe that was the answer! He turned to Helaine. "Check out your Book of Magic," he told her. "See if there's some spell in that which could work here."

"It's worth a try," agreed Helaine, a faint smile on her face. She fished her precious book from her pack, and started to look through it.

"How about a gateway?" suggested Score. "We could take Thunder back to Jewel. Or maybe even to Treen." Treen was the first world they had landed upon.

"I don't know," Pixel said doubtfully. "Can unicorns travel through gateways? We'd have to experiment first, and I don't think it would be wise to start with Thunder. He's already very sick."

Tychus snorted angrily. *I don't care what you do with him,* he thought. *As long as he's gone by sunset. Meanwhile . . .* He turned to face Nova and Flame. *All of the herd has sworn loyalty to me except the two of you. It is now your turn.*

Flame whirled around, her eyes blazing. *I'll *never* swear allegiance to you, you . . . you . . . *horse*!"

Pixel realized that this had to be one of the worst insults you could throw at another unicorn. Sort of like calling a person a monkey, he imagined. There was a gasp from the assembled herd, but Tychus only laughed.

If you will not swear to follow me, he snapped coldly, *then you, too, must leave the herd.* Pixel could hear a sneer in his words. *And a lone female out of herd land on her own is fair game for any rogue male who finds her.*

No! exclaimed Nova. Concern for her daughter

flooded from her. *You would not do that to her!*

Tychus shook his head in mock-sorrow. *You know the law. If she will not swear loyalty to me, she cannot be a part of the herd I lead. She must either take the oath, or leave our lands.*

Then I'll leave, Flame retorted angrily. *I won't follow the one who almost killed my father.*

Don't be so emotional about it, Tychus warned her. *You won't last long out there on your own. And what I did was according to the law. I cannot protect you unless you pledge yourself to me.*

Tychus is right, Nova broke in, unexpectedly. *You must do as he asks.*

Flame whirled to face her. *Mother!* she cried. *You cannot be serious! I will not do it.*

You will do as you are told! Nova thundered angrily. *You must be protected, and that means that you must stay with the herd. I know how little you like it — and, believe me, it hurts me, too — but this is the only way. You *must* pledge your loyalty to Tychus. *Now*.*

Flame shook her head stubbornly. *I won't do it. I'd sooner die.*

With a whinny of irritation and fear, Nova turned to Helaine. *Can't you talk some sense into her?* she begged. *She's your friend; make her see that she must do this thing, no matter how much she might dislike it.*

A thought came to Pixel, and he tapped Helaine on the shoulder. "Get out your agate," he said softly. "Can you use it so that only the five of us can talk to one another?"

Helaine was puzzled, but she removed the gem from her pouch. *Of course,* she sent back. *I assume you don't want this to be overheard, right?*

Right, he agreed. Pixel wasn't sure how he knew, but he'd had an idea. It was one of his talents, being able to put very little information together and make sense of it. *There's something very odd happening here,* he explained to Score, Flame, Nova, and Helaine. *Thunder's far more badly hurt than he should be. There's something about this fight that stinks. We need to have someone in the herd to keep an eye on Tychus, while the rest of us try and help Thunder. Flame, you *must* do as your mother asks. Stay with the herd and keep an eye on Tychus for us all.*

Flame choked for a moment, but then sounded hesitant. *I don't know if I can, all alone,* she admitted. *I'm scared, and I *hate* him.*

"You won't have to be alone,* Helaine said, stroking Flame's mane. *I'm sure Score, Pixel, and your mother can look after Thunder without our help.

I'll stay here with you.* She glared in the direction of Tychus. *And since I'm not a unicorn, he can't demand that I take an oath to serve him.*

He might try and expel you, Flame protested.

*He can *try*,* agreed Helaine. *But he won't live to finish it if he does, I'll promise you that. So, is it a deal?*

Sighing, Flame nodded. *Okay. I don't like it, but I'll do it.*

Fine, agreed Pixel. *Let's go back to speech, now.*

Helaine put her jewel away, and they turned to face Tychus.

All right, Flame said reluctantly. *I'll take the oath.* Pixel could hear the distaste in her voice, but she went down on her knees in front of the smug unicorn and promised to follow him loyally.

There, he said. *That wasn't so difficult, was it? Now you can stay with the herd.*

Helaine stepped forward. "And I'm staying with her, at least for a while," she said. "As I'm not a unicorn, I know you don't need me to swear allegiance to you. I have already given my word to the herd that I will do it no harm. That should be enough for you . . . shouldn't it?"

The unicorn who had earlier brought the subject up moved forward. *What she claims is true,* he said. *We have all agreed to allow them to come and go as they please, and they have pledged to act only in our best interests.*

Tychus glowered angrily. *But they have not pledged this to *me*,* he objected. *I am not bound by this . . . human-loving allegiance.*

"Maybe *you* aren't," Pixel said loudly. "But your herd is. And surely you'll support your herd?" He cocked his head to one side quizzically. He knew that Tychus was stuck. If he refused, then he was saying that he had become not their leader but their dictator, and that would be unacceptable to the herd.

Very well, he agreed ungraciously. *If the herd accepts you, then I accept you. But you had better be on your guard. If I find a cause, I shall expel you instantly from our company.*

"It's nice to be loved," joked Helaine.

Tychus turned back to Nova. *And now the last,* he said triumphantly. *It is your turn to pledge your allegiance to me. Not only as your leader, but as your new husband.*

"What?" exclaimed Pixel, hearing Helaine and Score echo his words with the same degree of shock and astonishment.

It is the law, Tychus announced coldly. *The old leader is replaced in *all* things by the new. That includes his marriage.*

Pixel realized what was going on. Tychus was sealing his place in the herd by wedding the old leader's wife. It was a common enough event in human history, too, legitimizing the claim to the throne. But how would Nova take it?

Nova stared at Tychus with undisguised contempt. *If you think I would wed the person who was about to kill my husband,* she answered, *then you're a bigger fool than I thought.*

You have no choice! cried Tychus, irritated by her refusal. *You *will* be my wife tonight.*

If I am your wife tonight, she retorted, *then I'll be your widow in the morning, I promise you that. Think carefully before you make that demand again, Tychus.* She stood there, staring angrily and disgustedly at him.

Tychus could obviously see her determination. Pixel knew that she was not bluffing: she was set to kill Tychus if she had to. And Tychus could see the same exact thing.

You cannot stay with the herd if you refuse this of me, he announced. *You must make a choice, here and now. Will you wed me, pledge your loyalty, and stay?*

No, Nova replied firmly. *I shall be where I belong: at the side of my husband.*

Very well, agreed Tychus. *Then, you, too, are

exiled from this herd. You must leave our lands by sundown, or else you will be killed. Do you understand?*

Perfectly, agreed Nova calmly.

Good. Tychus deliberately turned his back on them. *My herd!* he cried. *We return to the main pastures, immediately.* Glancing over his shoulder, he added: *We shall return at sunset. If either Thunder or Nova is still here, they are both to die. That is my decree, and as I ask it, so shall it happen.* With a whinny, he reared up, pawed the air, and then raced away.

The other unicorns followed after him. Only Flame lingered. She returned to her mother.

I'll go with him, too, she promised. *But I don't like this at all. Are you ready, Helaine? You'd better come with me.*

"Just a minute," Helaine answered. She had her Book of Magic open at a page which she showed to Pixel and Score. "This spell should do the trick," she told them. "It's a sort of mini-gateway, only instead of bridging the gap between two worlds, it makes a sort of tunnel between two places on the same world. The only thing is that you have to know exactly where you're going, and be able to form a very clear image of it in your mind. If you can't, then you can't go there."

Pixel nodded. "That sounds perfect." He glanced at Score. "How about the castle? If we take Thunder there, we can check if Garonath left any healing herbs or spells behind. And we both know what that looks like."

"Great," agreed Score. He grinned. "Don't they say something about a person's home being his castle? In our case, it seems like our castle is our home."

Together, they studied and memorized the spell. Then Helaine smiled sadly as she replaced the book in her bag.

"You know," she admitted, "I never thought I'd say this, but I'm going to miss the two of you. Just a few days ago, I'd have been glad to see you go. Now . . . Well, take care, okay?"

"You, too," Score said. "Despite everything, I've gotten used to you."

"So have I," agreed Pixel. He knew he was blushing, but he couldn't help it. "Try and stay out of trouble, will you?"

Helaine nodded. "I've still got the agate," she said. "I can always contact you telepathically if I need help." She gave a stiff nod and then vaulted onto Flame's back. "Let's go," she said gruffly. And then they were off, following the path the other unicorns had taken.

"Well," sighed Score. "It's time to get busy. Let's see if we can do this mini-gateway thing, shall we?"

Pixel nodded. "Let's focus our thoughts on the study in the castle," he said. "And then we can recite the spell together." He glanced at Nova. "It seems to be pretty localized, so you had better stand close to us." He put a hand on her mane, enjoying the feel of it in his fingers. Then he concentrated on forming a picture of the study in his mind. "Now," he said. He and Score recited the words of the spell together, concentrating all the time on the study . . . "*Ambrose ronica presant . . .*"

The world seemed to wrench about them. Pixel felt his stomach twist, as if he'd been punched. Lights flashed before his eyes. He almost collapsed. Only his grip on Nova's mane kept him upright. But when his vision cleared, he saw that they were now standing inside the study at the castle. Score had fallen to the floor and was shaking.

"That was *terrible,*" he complained. "Why didn't the book warn us that this would happen? I feel like I'm the one who fought Tychus and lost."

"It's obviously a very draining spell," Pixel agreed. "I can see it's not one we're going to use very often."

"Yeah." Score managed to struggle weakly back to his feet. "Well, there goes my idea of running a magic bus route. How do you feel, Nova?"

Fine, she answered. *It seems to have harmed only you magic-users. I'm sorry about that.*

"Well, it's gotten both of you off the herd land," Pixel answered, feeling some of his strength returning. "So that's the main thing." He staggered to a chair and collapsed into it. "I'm sure I'll feel better soon. Now, how's Thunder?"

Nova bent over her husband. *He's still delirious,* she replied. *But he's no worse off. He needs to be kept warm, and we should tend to his obvious injuries.*

Score nodded. "I'm sure we'll be able to find some medical supplies around here somewhere, though I don't know what kind of Band-Aids we'd use on a unicorn. Just give us a couple of minutes to catch our breath and we'll start looking."

It took more like fifteen minutes, but eventually they could both stand up without falling flat on their faces. "Let's split up," Pixel suggested. "If you find anything, yell out. I'll do the same." To Nova, he added: "You stay here with Thunder. We'll be as fast as we can."

"Yeah," agreed Score. "We should be back some time this century."

They both left the study. Pixel turned left and Score right. Pixel checked the first door he came to. It was obviously Garonath's old bedroom, with the bed still unmade. The man had been a slob. Pixel started to hunt through the chests on the floor, but they all contained only clothing. Then he heard Score give a faint yell. Pixel hurried out — at a speed an arthritic turtle could probably have beaten — and went after Score.

He'd found a bathroom of sorts, and was pulling medical supplies from a cupboard. "Bandages and herbal remedies," he explained. "There's some anti-infection cream. But I'm too weak to manage it on my own. You'll have to help me with it."

"I wish I could say it's no problem," Pixel answered. "But at the moment, I can't be sure of that." Still, together they managed to get enough strength to carry their finds back to the study.

There's no change, sighed Nova.

"This should help," Pixel told her. "Let us clean his wounds and dress them. He'll need to be kept warm. There's a bedroom next door. Do you think you could go and get some blankets from the bed? Right now, we're too weak to be able to manage it."

Of course. She trotted from the room.

Pixel collapsed to the floor beside Thunder. It felt good to be off his feet. Picking up the jar of anti-infection cream, he started to gently rub it into the gash in Thunder's shoulder. Then he stopped, frowning. "What's this?" he asked, puzzled.

“What’s what?” Score peered over Thunder’s neck from where he was doing the same task with the smaller cut.

“Here, where Tychus’s horn gouged Thunder,” Pixel explained, pointing to the edges of the cut. There was a faint trace of white grains in the cut.

Score bent forward, and licked his finger. He used it to pick up a few grains of the stuff and then sniffed it. “It’s some kind of drug!” he exclaimed. “So *that’s* what happened!”

What did? asked Nova, returning pulling the blankets in her teeth.

“Tychus brushed some sort of drug on his horn,” Pixel said coldly. “All he needed to do was to cut Thunder with the tip of his horn to get the drug into his bloodstream. That’s why Thunder collapsed without any real reason. Tychus cheated and drugged him!”

CHAPTER 4

Score was furious. Tychus hadn't won the fight fairly at all! He'd resorted to trickery to do it. And he would have killed Thunder if it hadn't been for their intervention. "I think it's time to go and fix him," he snarled.

No, said Nova firmly.

"Huh?" Score couldn't believe what she was thinking. "Tychus *cheated*, and he almost killed Thunder. Surely we have to go and tell the truth and get Tychus thrown out?"

It's not that simple, Nova replied with a sigh. *Tychus is now the herd leader, even if he cheated. The herd has sworn to follow him. The only way out is if someone challenges him to Rite of Combat and defeats him. Obviously, Thunder isn't up to that. The next time, we can check for cheating, but it's too late now. Besides which, there is only *your* word so far that Thunder was drugged. I'm sure Tychus will claim that you two put the drug there to frame him. And we can't prove otherwise right now.*

Score knew that she was right, but he couldn't just give up. "You mean that, even knowing Tychus was a cheat and a fraud, the herd would follow him?"

They have no option, Nova answered. *They have given their oath, and unicorns do not go back on their given words. They would hope for someone to challenge Tychus, certainly, or maybe one of them might do it. But there's no guarantee of that.*

Shaking his head, Score grumbled: "So you want us to do *nothing*, then?"

Not quite, Nova replied. *We have to get Thunder well again. When he's recovered, he can challenge Tychus to a return fight. And *we* will make certain that Tychus doesn't cheat next time.*

Pixel sighed. "I don't much like it," he said, "but it's about the only plan we've got right now." He looked down at Thunder. "Do you think he'll recover quickly, Nova?"

He's very strong, she answered with pride.

He'll probably be fine in the morning. Then just a few days to rest up from the wounds and I'm sure he'll be ready to tear Tychus apart.

"Okay," Score agreed. But he shook his head. "I still don't like the idea of doing nothing, though. I'd rather be taking Tychus on and showing him he can't get away with what he's done, even for just a short while. I'm sure he's up to something, even as we speak." He helped Pixel cover Thunder with the blankets. Nova settled down beside her husband.

The two of you should get some food, she told them. *And some rest. That teleportation tired you both out. Perhaps later we can talk some more.*

"Yes, Mother," Score answered cheekily, a little of his good humor returning. Things were bad right now, but they would get better. As long as Thunder was okay, there wouldn't be any problem. He looked down at his friend, who lay on the floor, eyes closed, nostrils dilating slightly as he breathed. He *would* be all right. He *had* to be . . .

Thunder was very confused. It seemed to him that he was standing in the unicorn fields, looking north. Everything seemed unusually still, though, and there didn't seem to be any sounds. His ears flickered, but there was nothing. No birds singing, no insects buzzing, not even the sigh of a breeze.

What was he doing here? He could remember that there had been a Rite of Combat. And he knew that he must have lost; he'd certainly recall if he had won. But if that was the case, what was he doing here like this?

He turned around, sniffing for any scent of other unicorns, but he could smell nothing. Nor was there anyone in sight. Not even those humans he was actually beginning to like. It was very odd.

Hello, Thunder, came an old, familiar voice. Thunder spun around and stared in amazement at the unicorn that was mildly watching him from a clump of bushes. He hadn't been there a minute earlier, Thunder knew. Then he gasped with astonishment as he recognized the newcomer. He was a large, white unicorn with a black star-shaped splash on his forehead, just below his horn. That patch had given him his name.

Darkstar! exclaimed Thunder. *Is it really you, after all these years?*

Me? Yes, Darkstar said with a gentle laugh. *Really? No. I'm not physically here, back on the old fields. Neither are you, old friend.*

I was in a Rite of Combat, Thunder explained, puzzled. *I rather think I must have lost.*

You were and you did, agreed Darkstar. *With Tychus. I know him, that one. He was responsible for my fate, too.*

Yours? Thunder blinked and snorted. *What did he do to you?* His eyes narrowed. *Are you . . . a ghost?* Then, with a sudden, sick dread: *Am *I* dead?*

We're neither of us dead, Darkstar answered. *Though I've often wished I were. I've been dreaming these past five years. Suddenly, I became aware of your mind. This is very hard for me, and I can't keep it up very long. Tychus defeated you by drugging you. It sent your mind whirling, and you could no longer control your body. But the drug had a side effect. It has increased your telepathic ability for a short while, and your mind has overlapped mine. But I must hurry. Don't interrupt me!* he added quickly. *I must get through this before I grow too weak.

You must come after me and find me. I am to the north. There are directions I left behind on the Horn Rock. Follow them and you will find me. Then I can explain everything.

Thunder nodded, even though he wasn't sure what this all meant. *I will do as you say,* he promised.

Good. Darkstar was growing faint, fading like a

breeze. *I have used all my strength. Come to me, Thunder. Come to me!* His voice faded out, and he was gone, leaving Thunder alone on the unicorn field again.

He didn't know what to make of this. Was this real? Or was it some sort of hallucination? Darkstar had mentioned something about a drug. That would explain how Tychus had managed to win, and why Thunder felt so odd. But did it also explain the vision? Was he just imagining all of this?

Well, there was a simple way to find out the truth: go to Horn Rock. If there were directions there, then he would know this had not been an illusion.

Thunder snorted suddenly. There was an odd feeling all through him. Like something had died and was rotting close by. His nostrils flared and he looked around.

Tychus was watching him from the shade of a large, orange tree. There was a feeling of *wrongness* about him, as if something had been warped. Thunder couldn't tell what it was, but there was something very peculiar about Tychus indeed.

So, the crimson unicorn growled, *you're still alive, after all? Well, it'll do you no good. I've defeated you, Thunder, and your herd now belongs to me. You don't stand a chance of getting it back.*

Thunder pawed the ground and snorted loudly. *You cheated to defeat me,* he answered. *You drugged me to win the fight. It will not happen again.*

Tychus laughed. *You're thinking that you can challenge me again and this time defeat me?* he asked. *Thunder, that drug was just the first of my tricks. I defeated Darkstar and I can defeat you, too, no matter what you try. And the next time, I shall not allow you to live. Be sensible, old fool: stay away from me and you'll be safe.*

You are a cheat and a fraud, Thunder said. *When I became leader of the herd, your kind was one of the menaces I pledged to root out and destroy. I shall not stop now, just because you threaten me.*

It is no longer your herd, Tychus said coldly. *It is *my* herd now. Their welfare is no longer your concern.*

It is, Thunder replied. *I cannot abandon them when they need me. We shall face one another again soon, Tychus. And I promise you — this time you will not be victorious.*

Fool, Tychus snarled. *Face me again and you die. I make you that promise. There is *nothing* you can do that will defeat me.* Then he whirled around and was gone.

Thunder stared after him for a moment, and then

reared up, pawing the air. *Run!* he cried out. *But I shall find you again — and defeat you!*

Score awoke feeling as if he'd been run over by an angry dragon. Every muscle in his body ached. That spell-casting had really done a number on him. It was definitely a spell he wouldn't be reusing in a hurry. Blinking, he looked around himself, trying to get his bearings.

He was in a small chamber in one of the turrets, he realized. He could barely remember finding the room last night — at least, he *hoped* that it had been last night; it could have been days ago — and now the morning sunlight was streaming through the room's small window. It was a room that hadn't been used in a while, and he'd found some spare bedding there. No bed — after all, the late owner hadn't exactly encouraged visitors. So he'd made a pile of clothing on the floor into a bed.

Well, at least he was now awake. What he needed was a bath and food. Climbing wearily to his feet, Score staggered out of the room. If he recalled properly, there had been a room with a bath in it on the way back to the study. He tried doors as he went, and found the room on his third attempt.

Pixel was just getting dressed there. There was a big stone tub behind him, with steaming water draining from it. "Morning, sleepyhead," he said with a grin. "You managed to find your way here, then?"

"Yeah," Score agreed. "I figured a hot bath might help my aching muscles." He shook his head in amazement. "But I can't believe that Garonath had one rigged up."

"Well, you have to cheat a bit," Pixel replied. His water had drained, and he replaced the stopper in the bottom of the tub. He indicated a sloping chute that came down from the ceiling, with a pull-cord attached. "He's got a rainwater collector on the roof for water," he explained. "Pull the cord, and it comes into the bath. But it's ice-cold."

"Ice-cold isn't what I need right now," Score grunted.

"Then do what I did," Pixel advised him. "A fire-spell warms it up very fast."

Score grinned, and held out his chrysolite. "You're forgetting I have power over Water," he said. "I was going to heat it like that. And if there wasn't any water, I could just condense it from the air into the tub."

Pixel whistled, impressed. "You're really starting to get the hang of this magic game, aren't you?"

"We have to," Score said. "It's the only way we'll survive. Anyway, have you thought about breakfast?"

"I've thought about very little else since I woke up," Pixel admitted. "I know there's a kitchen around here somewhere. I'll see if I can't whip something up while you take your bath. I'll meet you with whatever I find in the study when you're done."

"It's a deal," agreed Score. He was really getting used to having friends around, too, he realized. As Pixel headed off after food, Score pulled the cord over his head, and let the water flow into the tub. Then, using his gemstone, he heated the water until it was just the right temperature. He plunged into the tub and sat back for a good soak.

After about fifteen minutes, his muscles felt less tense and knotted. He grabbed his clothes, which were pretty dirty by now, and washed them out in the tub. Then, using the chrysolite, he made all of the water in his clothes evaporate, leaving them absolutely dry. Grinning, he stepped out of the bath, and then used the gemstone on himself. "Better than a towel," he decided, happy with this new trick. Dressing quickly, he left the bathwater to drain and started back for the study. He was still a little sore, but a lot better than before. He was also ravenously hungry.

Pixel was there already, with two plates. He was making inroads in his own, and gestured Score to the other. Score checked Nova and Thunder first, but both unicorns were sleeping. Thunder seemed to be more relaxed, and he was breathing steadily, so Score headed for breakfast. Pixel had managed to find some thick slabs of bread. Score complemented these by conjuring up a couple of scrambled eggs and some sort of meat. The only implement to eat with was a flat knife. Pixel was using his to cut the food, and then as a sort of spoon to eat with, so Score copied him.

When they had finished, Score went with Pixel back to the kitchen, where they stashed the dirty dishes in a tub. "There's a fair amount of food in a pantry," Pixel explained, gesturing to a door. "It's in good shape, so it will last us for a couple of weeks, I would think."

Score grinned. "I'm getting kind of used to this place already," he admitted. "Maybe we can all move in here. Let's face it, it must seem like home to Helaine. It just needs a bit of tidying up and some personalizing."

"It's not a bad idea," agreed Pixel. "We're going to have to stay somewhere, so why not here? Besides, we're magic-users now, and most magic-users seem to live in castles. We have standards to uphold."

Laughing, Score led the way back to the study. He felt quite at ease with Pixel. It was hard to remember that he'd originally thought the other boy was a total dork. And even Helaine wasn't so bad; he'd liked her praise yesterday, and she was getting a lot less uptight. Maybe there was something to this friendship business, after all.

As he entered the study, Score saw that Thunder's eyes were flickering. Then they opened. Hurrying forward, Score called: "Thunder! How do you feel!"

Why am I lying here? Thunder demanded. He rolled from his side to his knees, and then stood up. Score was astonished that he could move at all, let alone so easily. Nova had been quite right — Thunder was one tough customer.

His movement had wakened Nova. She blinked and then stared at her husband. *Thunder! Are you all right?*

Perfectly, Thunder answered, tossing his head. *My thoughts are clear once again, and that poison of Tychus's has gone from my body. I'm my old self again.*

"That's the spirit!" Score said happily. He rubbed Thunder's nose. "It's great to see you back on your feet again. We were so worried about you."

Thunder snorted. *Yes. It would have been embarrassing to have had to remove a dead unicorn from the room, wouldn't it?*

Thunder, Nova cautioned him. *There's no

need to be rude. They saved your life yesterday when Tychus was going to kill you.*

Thunder looked at Score and then at Pixel and then sighed. *Then that means I owe you for it,* he stated. *And I always pay my debts. But why did it have to be *humans* who saved me?*

"To teach you a bit of tolerance," answered Score, grinning. He knew that Thunder didn't really mean to sound so grouchy; it was just his normal manner. "After all, all of your herd has sworn allegiance to Tychus."

Nova filled her husband in on what had happened after he had been defeated, nuzzling him fondly as she did so. When she was done, Thunder nodded.

Good thinking, he approved. *And with Flame and Helaine with the herd, we'll be able to keep tabs on what Tychus is up to.*

"And as soon as your strength's back," Score said enthusiastically, "you can challenge Tychus again. This time, we'll check him out for dirty tricks before the return bout. He won't win by trickery again. So, how long do you figure? One day? Two?"

It isn't that simple, Thunder replied. *I might not be facing him for a while.*

"What?" Score couldn't believe what he was hearing. "Don't tell me you're *scared*!"

Thunder's head whirled, and his horn stopped inches away from Score's heart. *Don't *ever* say anything like that again,* Thunder snapped. *If you hadn't saved my life, I wouldn't have held back.*

"Boy, touchy, aren't you?" complained Score. "Okay, I'm sorry I said it. Now, *why* aren't you facing him again then?"

Because there is something else I must do first. Thunder told them about his dream, and finished: *I have to listen to Darkstar. He has never led me astray. We have to find him first.*

Score shook his head in disbelief. "You have a dream that tells you to go chasing dead unicorns, and you're going to do it?" he asked. "Maybe we should get you to a unicorn psychiatrist. This is crazy."

I know what happened, Thunder replied. *And I am convinced that it is real. I will do as Darkstar requested and try and find him.*

"This is loopy," complained Score. "Isn't it, guys?" he asked Pixel and Nova.

"It sounds pretty far-fetched," agreed Pixel. "But so does almost everything that's happened to us this past week or so. What's one more miracle among the lot?"

And, besides, added Nova. *It's very simple to check. We go to Horn Rock and see if there is a message. If there is, Thunder's dream was right. If there isn't, we won't have wasted much time. The rock's only half a day from here.*

Score shrugged. "Well, if you both think it's worth it, I guess I'll go along with you for now. But it still sounds pretty flakey to me." He eyed Thunder suspiciously. "You're very quiet. Is there something you're not telling us?"

Well . . . the unicorn said reluctantly. *The Horn Rock is on the herd's land.*

"Oh, *great*," muttered Score. "This *is* the same herd that's threatened to kill you if you trespass, right?" He threw his hands up in bewilderment. "And I had started to think that this was a pretty good day. I must have been out of my skull. You're going to get us killed, you know that?"

Then I shall go alone, Thunder answered simply.

NO! yelled Nova. The two humans were a shade slower in saying the same thing.

"We're in this together," Score stated firmly. "I may think you're dumb and that this is suicide. But we'll all be dumb and suicidal together. No arguments." He rolled his eyes. "That's it. After this, I'm going back to New York to hire a really good analyst. I *must* be going crazy to agree to this."

He was making a joke out of it, but it only was to cover his nerves. Tychus was bound to have unicorns out watching to see if Thunder tried to sneak back.

They were heading into real trouble, he was certain. So why wasn't he doing the smart thing and waiting back here at the castle for them?

Because they were his friends. Score had *known* it was a mistake to make friends. They only got you into trouble. And, in this case, probably killed . . .

CHAPTER 5

Helaine was worried. Badly worried. She had hoped that spending her time with the unicorns would cheer her up and remove her air of gloomy foreboding. After all, she loved Flame, and unicorns seemed to have a good effect on her in general. There was just something so noble, so regal, so *right* about the creatures. They were beautiful, alert, and fun to be around.

Normally.

But these weren't normal times. There was a terrible tension hanging over the whole herd. Thunder had been a bit cranky at times, but there was no question that he had been a good and popular leader. Everyone was missing him. They were embarrassed that he had been beaten, and had needed to be saved by humans. The unicorns' dislike of humans had been formed a long time ago.

Wizards had hunted unicorns down for hundreds of years. They did this because unicorn horns negated all forms of magic. All any unicorn had to do was to somehow charge their horns up, and they could use them to drain magic away. This made the possession of a unicorn horn tremendously valuable to magicians. They could use them then to counter the spells of other wizards. And the only way to get a unicorn horn was by killing its owner. The unicorns were understandably very alarmed by this.

But Helaine, Pixel, and Score had no such desire for a horn. They all loved the unicorns for what they were, and wouldn't dream of hurting one of them. Thunder had been reluctant to believe this at first, but Flame had known it to be the truth from the start. She and Helaine had bonded, and were now firm friends. Thunder, and then the rest of his herd, had eventually accepted the trio. But they were still cautious about humans. Prejudice is hard to eliminate overnight. So the herd tended to shy away from Helaine, just enough to be uncomfortable.

The unicorns felt bad for Flame, but they didn't know what to say or do to make her feel better. So they were avoiding her, too. All except a young male named Dustdevil. He was Flame's age, and was gray with black and white flecks. The two of them were great friends; it was clear he wouldn't abandon her. But he couldn't cheer her up, either.

It was Flame's depression that hurt Helaine the most. Flame was normally the most cheerful unicorn in the herd. But with her father and mother banished, and the rest of the herd pretty much avoiding her, Flame's mood had plummeted to rock bottom. She moped, refusing to eat or to take part in any of the herd's activities. Nothing Helaine could say or do helped. To be honest, she felt pretty much the same way herself.

Still, she had no option but to stay. She had to keep an eye on Flame, and she had to try to figure out what Tychus was up to.

It was early in the morning, but the new herd leader had been up since dawn. He had wakened several of the younger males, as Helaine had listened in.

Up! he had cried. *I need you to go out on patrols. Keep on the move and check the perimeter of our lands. If Thunder or Nova attempt to return here, do not challenge them, but return to tell me immediately.*

Why would either seek to return? one unicorn asked, puzzled. *You would surely just defeat him again?*

Because Thunder's pride has been hurt by his defeat, Tychus explained. *He wants to oust me and reclaim the herd again. But he knows he can't defeat me in a fair fight, so he will seek to raise suspicions against me, and to do everything he can to undermine my authority. Do not speak with him or his wife. If you see them, come immediately to fetch me. I shall force him to depart again — or die!*

Thunder would never do that, Helaine thought to herself. He was much too straightforward and honest to try to lie and cheat. Then why would Tychus claim otherwise? Was it just because he disliked the deposed leader? Or was it because Thunder knew something? Maybe something true about Tychus that might make the other unicorns reject their new leader? Why else order them not to speak to Thunder?

Tychus was up to something, Helaine realized. Now, more than before, it was important that she discover what it was and fix it. Tychus had a plan. He clearly expected Thunder to return. Which meant that he had some way of knowing that Thunder was okay. That was a relief. Helaine fished her agate from her pack and held it clenched in her hand. *Pixel,* she thought clearly. *Can you hear me?*

Ouch . . . Loud and clear, he replied. *Very loud, in fact. What's wrong?*

Sorry, she apologized, slightly toning down the

power she was using. *Tychus is sending out sentries to patrol the fields. He seems to think that Thunder is going to try to sneak back.*

There was a slight pause, and then Pixel admitted: *He is. We have to check something out.* He brought Helaine up to date on what they were doing. *So, we're going to have to try it anyway. We need to know if what Thunder saw was a message, or just a delusion.*

Well, watch out, Helaine answered. *I'll contact you again later.* She put the jewel away and then went to Flame. "Tychus cheated," she said bluntly. "That's how he beat your father." Then she explained everything to Flame and Dustdevil.

We have to tell everyone this, Dustdevil said.

"It's no good," Helaine replied. "They won't believe us. We have no proof to back up what we say. Do you *really* think the herd will believe two foals and a human?"

No, agreed Flame. But the fire had come back into her spirit now. Knowing that her father had been beaten only by a trick had made her angry. *But we know the truth. If Tychus is a liar and a cheat, he's going to make a mistake, and we should be able to catch him and expose him. We need to look for the opportunity.* She laughed and tossed her head.

*And if he *does* make a slip, I'll pounce on it in a second.*

Helaine smiled. This was what Flame had needed. She had believed that her father had been beaten fairly, and that there was nothing that she could do. Now that she knew the truth, however, she had a mission. Helaine almost felt sorry for Tychus. "So let's go and see what he's up to," she suggested.

They found him in the central meadow, with almost all of the younger unicorns around him. Not the foals, who were either playing or with their mothers, but the young male and female adults.

In the past, Tychus was informing them, *you were never given much to do. Your parents and the other older unicorns reserved all of the good things for themselves, telling you that you would have to wait for later to do these things. Well, I don't believe in that. I believe that any productive member of the herd should be rewarded. All of you will be equal in my sight. And if you can do what is needed for the herd better than those who are older than you — well, I will not favor age. To show I mean what I say . . .* He turned to one of the silvered unicorns. *Moondust, you will be one of my assistants. I've been asking around, and everyone says that you're one of the bravest, smartest, and most loyal in the herd. The only reason you've never been given any responsibility in the past is because you were considered too young. I think that's a foolish reason. As long as you can do your job well, you will have it.*

Moondust stepped proudly forward, beaming his pleasure. *Thank you, Tychus. I promise you won't regret this decision. I'll help you in any way I can.*

I know I won't regret it, Tychus agreed. *You'll make me proud of you, I'm certain of that.*

Helaine snorted. "He's promoting the younger unicorns, making them think they're valuable," she explained to Flame and Dustdevil. "This way, they'll be loyal to him, knowing that if Thunder did come back, they'd lose their new status. And he's making certain that anyone who might still harbor affection for Thunder is no longer in a position of influence. Oh, he's smart — and evil."

I don't care how smart he is, Flame replied. *I know that the three of us will be able to expose him as a fraud.*

Helaine hoped that this was true. She watched as Tychus gave two of the other youngsters a promotion, and then sent them out to work. These unicorns were still young enough not to be able to hide their feelings too well, and she could feel the pride, happiness, and smugness radiating from them. Tychus was planning well, getting them onto his side. It wouldn't be a simple matter to turn them against him.

And now, Tychus added, *we have further things to do.* He looked at where Flame, Dustdevil and Helaine were standing. *You three, come here.*

Uh-oh . . . Helaine had a bad feeling about this. There was no way that Tychus was going to feel terribly kindly toward either her or Flame. And Dustdevil had made a declaration of where he stood by being seen publicly with both of them. Still, there was no avoiding this issue. She strode forward, head held high. She was a Lady of Ordin, and there was no way that she would behave in any other fashion. Flame trotted at her side. A little less self-confident, Dustdevil trailed slightly behind them.

Tychus eyed them as they halted in front of him. He was physically intimidating, but Helaine didn't let that sway her. He couldn't read her thoughts unless she used the agate, and that remained safely in her pouch. She was going to give nothing away to him.

But his first look was directed at Flame. *Daughter of Thunder,* he said, making sure the assembled young unicorns could hear him. *Because of your father, in the past you had a position of privilege. This can no longer be allowed.*

Privilege? Flame snorted. *My father treated me like a *child*. I had no rights, so there's nothing you can take away from me.*

You mistake my intention, Tychus said fluidly. *I will not punish you for the accident of your birth. Within my herd, everyone is equal. There will be no favoritism.*

That's a joke, thought Helaine to herself. He was doing nothing *but* playing favorites. Only he didn't want that to be too obvious.

You will be given duties to perform, Tychus added to Flame. *If you do them well and cheerfully, you will have as much chance of promotion and honor as any other in the herd.* He turned to Dustdevil. *The same applies to you, too. All I ask of anyone is that they devote themselves to the service of the herd. If they do that, then they will be rewarded. Do you both think this is possible for you? Or will you refuse to help the herd?*

It was nicely done, Helaine had to admit. Tychus was giving them extra work, but making it look like a refusal was a rejection of the herd.

*Whatever the *herd* needs, I will be proud to do,* Flame answered, stressing the word very clearly.

That is all I ask, Tychus answered glibly. *Your duties will be assigned to you shortly. First, however, there is a less pleasant task to perform.* He now turned to face Helaine, and she realized that the confrontation had arrived. *Humans are not welcome on unicorn lands.*

"I was accepted by the herd," Helaine said clearly. "I have been accorded the right to be here."

That was before I took the mantle of leadership, Tychus replied. *Thunder may have enjoyed fraternizing with humans, but I am not as foolish as he. I recall all of the terrible things that humans have done to unicorns in the past. Humans *kill* unicorns.*

Helaine shook her head. "I have given my word to help the herd," she said. "I will never harm a unicorn."

*So *you* say,* sneered Tychus. *But can we believe the word of a *human*? And,* he added, before any reply could be made, *it is not just you that we must consider. Where one, or two, or three humans now walk, soon there will be more. *Perhaps* this human has no animosity toward the herd, but can she speak for all who will follow her? Others *will* come. It is inevitable. Humans cannot be trusted, and the only way to make the herd safe is to banish her and all other humans.*

"Nonsense," Helaine snapped. "There are only the three of us. There will be no more."

"Oh," said an all-too-familiar voice. "Did I come at a bad time?"

Helaine groaned and turned to see Oracle looking at her. "What do *you* want?"

There will be no more humans? mocked Tychus. *And then one arrives. She has just *proven* that she cannot be trusted. Do you need more proof?*

"He's *not* human!" Helaine snarled. "He just *looks* like one."

Well, he's certainly not a unicorn! snorted Tychus.

Helaine stepped forward and thrust her hand through Oracle's body. The unicorns gasped as they saw this. "He's just a projection," she explained patiently. "He's not exactly real. Or very bright, either. What are you doing here?"

"I came to warn you about trouble," Oracle answered. "It's starting to look like that is redundant."

She's been proven a liar once! Tychus exclaimed. *We must drive her from the pastures before she brings further trouble!* He lunged forward at Helaine with his horn.

Her reaction was pure instinct. Her sword was out, in her hands, and held at the ready before she could even consciously think about it.

Ha! cried Tychus, stopping short. *And she said that she would *never* harm a unicorn! Yet she draws a weapon on me! As I insisted, you cannot trust a human. Banish her!*

Realizing she'd been manipulated, Helaine re-sheathed her sword. "I thought you were attacking me!" she protested. "I was just defending myself."

Another of your lies, Tychus sneered. Helaine could see that the other unicorns were leaning toward his side. *We must drive her out, in order to be safe from her and other humans.*

That did it. Helaine had been restraining her temper, but she couldn't allow herself to be driven away. Who would look after Flame? She took the chrysoprase from her bag. This gave her control over the element of Earth. "You had better let me be," she said, showing the gem. "You know that I am a magic-user. I can turn the Earth itself against you if you try to harm me."

*We do not intend to *harm* you,* Tychus said glibly. *We just want you gone from our lands.* He looked around. *To me, unicorns,* he called. *Surround her with your horns. That will prevent her from using her magic.*

The young unicorns started to obey him. Circling Helaine, their horns started to glow as they began to make them ready to counter her magic. Helaine knew that if she was going to use her gemstone, she would have to do it quickly, before they had her enveloped. But she couldn't do it. She liked these creatures, and they weren't actually trying to harm her. True, they were acting on the wrong assumptions, but she couldn't bring herself to harm them just because of that. Reluctantly, she replaced the gem in her pouch. She was now surrounded by the young unicorns. She could sense that her magical abilities were now at zero. Even with the crystals, she could do nothing.

You have prevented her from acting, Tychus said proudly. *Now, drive her from our lands. She must never be allowed to return.*

"All right," Helaine said, with as much strength as she could muster. "I'll go. I have no choice, except to harm some of you, and that I won't do. But let me tell you this." She glared at the unicorns. "I am not the danger to your herd. Nor are other humans. *He* is." She pointed at Tychus. "Weigh everything he tells you very carefully, because he will lie, promise, and cheat you to get what he wants."

*Are you quite finished, *human*?* Tychus demanded. *Then go, and take that whatever-it-is with you. And if we see your face here again, you will be killed.*

Helaine turned from him, giving Flame a tremulous smile, and then marched toward the encircling unicorns. They parted, allowing her and Oracle to leave. She didn't look back, because that would have been too hard. She simply walked, heading for Garonath's old castle. There wasn't much else she could do right now. She could feel the eyes of all of the unicorns on her back, which made her very uneasy.

"Congratulations," she told Oracle dryly. "You turned up at the worst possible moment. How do you manage such impeccable timing?"

"It's a gift, I suppose," he answered, shrugging. "I'm sorry that I caused you problems, but I did come with the best of intentions."

"I'm sure you did," she agreed. "So what were they?"

"Well, I was visiting Shanara, and the two of us did some spell work to see what was wrong here on Dondar."

"And what did you learn?" asked Helaine.

"Nothing."

"Nothing?" she echoed.

"Zero. Zip. Nada." Oracle shrugged.

Helaine was having difficulty keeping her temper. "And you came here to tell me *that*?" she demanded.

"It's very important," Oracle protested. "You know how strong Shanara is, especially when Blink helps her out. There's only one way that she could discover nothing on this planet at all. And that's if there's another wizard around who's stronger than her and blocking her."

Helaine started to get the point. "You mean, then, that this business with Tychus and the unicorns isn't the *real* problem here," she said slowly. "That there's another wizard at work, and it's his or her plan that's causing trouble."

"Exactly," Oracle agreed happily. "This Tychus is just a minor player in this game. There's somebody much more powerful for you to worry about."

Helaine sighed heavily. "And you think that's *good* news?" she asked. She shook her head. "We're in bigger trouble than I imagined."

CHAPTER 6

Pixel watched the woods around them warily. It was still a bit odd seeing purple trees and blue grass, but he liked it. Besides, it wasn't that much crazier than some of the worlds he'd created in Virtual Reality. Only this one was *real*, and he was walking it with unicorns that were equally real . . . and, with Tychus's guards out, potentially dangerous. "Will you be able to spot any other unicorns telepathically?" he asked Nova.

She shook her head. *Telepathy for us is like talking for you,* she explained. *If one of us doesn't want to be heard, we won't be. That's how I can whisper to you without Thunder overhearing.*

*I heard *that*,* Thunder commented. *My own wife, talking behind my back, to a *human*. What is the world coming to?*

"Says you," Score pointed out with a grin, "talking to another human."

"So we've just got to be cautious and keep a good look-out?" asked Pixel. Nova nodded.

"How about using your ruby?" suggested Score.

Pixel sighed. "It won't work on unicorns," he answered. Normally, he could use his ruby to locate anything. "Their horns negate the gem's powers. These unicorns *know* we're magic-users, so they'll be ready to combat us. Any magic we try from here on in will be useless against them."

"You're really not doing a lot to cheer me up," Score complained.

"How do you think *I* feel?" asked Pixel. "The unicorn scouts will be able to locate us by following the sound of my knees knocking together." But he couldn't give up and abandon his friends, and he knew that Score felt the same way. Bravery wasn't very easy, but it was better than cowardice.

We're at the edge of the herd lands now, Thunder said softly. *I think we had better keep very silent from now on, until we reach the Horn Rock. Not even any loud thoughts!* Then he led the way across the small stream that marked the boundary, and through the orange-colored trees on the far shore.

Walking in silence was even worse. Pixel's eyes flickered all around, looking for any sign of the scouts. His ears strained to hear anything out of the ordinary. The problem was that he wasn't too sure what was ordinary for these woods. Alien worlds tended to be very different from anything he'd known before, and an odd sound could be anything from an insect chirping to a monster getting ready to attack. But at least there shouldn't be any monsters. One of the herd leader's jobs was to keep the herd lands free from trouble.

So all he had to worry about was being attacked by unicorns. He couldn't help eyeing Nova's horn, and imagining the kind of damage it could do to a human body if it hit . . . He shuddered, conjured up all of his courage, and carried on walking.

Pixel was still very uncertain about what was going on. Why had Tychus taken the risky step of drugging Thunder? The maneuver could have backfired on him. Why did he want control of the herd so badly? He was obviously expecting trouble. It didn't make much sense to Pixel, but he supposed that the answer could be that Tychus simply wanted power. It was something that a lot of humans desired, even if Pixel didn't.

Thunder had said that the Horn Rock wasn't very far in on unicorn land. After just five minutes, Pixel could make out a small clearing ahead. As they drew closer, he could see that there was a large rock in the center of the clearing. It was about four feet across, and around fifteen feet tall. It was indeed shaped like a unicorn horn, and it was quite obviously an artificial construction. Pixel had read about ancient civilizations that used to make these kinds of things. They were called *menhirs.* But there were very few humans on Dondar — actually, three right now — and just as few in the past. Had this stone been raised by a human, or by one of the intelligent nonhuman species? It was something to ask Nova later.

Just as they were about to step into the clearing, a chocolate-brown unicorn specked with white stepped from hiding and blocked their way. Pixel jumped, and his heart started to race.

Thunder, the unicorn thought loudly, *coming back here was a very foolish move.*

Thunder whinnied. *I had no choice, Cloud,* he replied. *Tychus cheated to defeat me. I must regain my herd. Are you now standing against me?*

I pledged to be loyal to him, Cloud answered. *And I am to report to him when I see you.* He paused. *So I'd better go and tell him that I've seen you.* He turned, and then smiled. *If I walk fast, I should be back to tell him in about fifteen minutes. That had better be long enough for you to do whatever you're planning.*

"He's helping you," breathed Pixel.

He was always a friend, answered Thunder simply. *He is keeping his oath, but giving me a chance. Come on!* He hurried up to the rock, the others just behind him. *There!* he exclaimed. *My vision was not wrong!*

Pixel studied the stone, and had to agree with Thunder. There was indeed a message. But what did it *mean*?

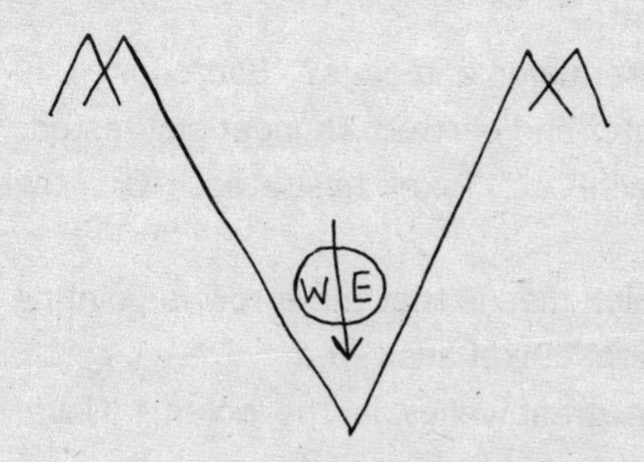

"We?" Pixel asked, pointing to the letters carved in the stone.

It means as much to me as it does to you, Thunder admitted sadly.

"Which isn't very much," Score observed.

"It's *we* inside a V," Pixel said.

"But what are these?" Score asked, pointing to the edges of the V.

Mountains, Nova answered. *They look like mountains made of ice.*

"Yes!" Pixel agreed. "Which means the V is a valley. Right?"

Nova nodded.

"But what does the *we* mean?" Score wondered aloud. "We already know that we're the ones who are supposed to find Darkstar. How does this help us?"

"What if the *we* isn't a *we*?" Pixel asked. "Look at the arrow. Maybe the W and the E are supposed to be separate."

"Watermelon and eggs?" Score joked.

Water and earth? Thunder suggested.

"Maybe . . ." Pixel hesitated. "Or . . . west and east."

Which means that the arrow is pointing —

"North," Pixel answered.

The great valley in the north, Nova nodded. *Within the range of ice and snow.*

"North it is," agreed Score. "But maybe we'd better hurry? Tychus could be along at any moment."

A good thought, agreed Nova, nervously. *We've used up most of the time that Cloud gave us.* She eyed Pixel. *I think we might be better off sacrificing subtlety for speed now. Climb on my back.*

Pixel was amazed. "I didn't think you liked to be ridden," he said.

I don't, much, she agreed. *But we'll travel faster if the two of you ride.*

Wonderful! grumbled Thunder. *Now I have to act like a *horse*.* He gave a theatrical sigh. *Sometimes I wonder if it's all worth it.* Then he glared at Score. *Well, what are you waiting for? Get on!*

Pixel scrambled up onto Nova, as Score did the same with Thunder. *Hold onto my mane,* Nova instructed him. *Unless you're a really good rider, this could get rough.*

"I'm not," Pixel admitted. "I've only ridden a horse once before. And never a unicorn."

Well, relax, Nova answered. *We're much more intelligent than horses. But it'll still be bumpy.* And then she sprang forward.

Pixel wound his hands into her mane and clung on for dear life. Thunder and Score were just behind them as they set off, and Nova ran back down the path they had walked earlier.

There they are! came a furious cry from behind them. Pixel craned his neck as far round as he dared, and saw that there were five other unicorns bursting into the clearing. None of them was Cloud or Tychus though. *After them!*

The next few minutes were a nightmare. Nova kept her head down and ran hard. She did her best to dodge obstacles, but her weaving about didn't help Pixel to stay in place. It was hard to keep his balance; riding a unicorn bareback was a very sore experience. He was torn between keeping his eyes shut to avoid panicking and keeping them open to see what was ahead. The ride was furious.

He glanced back, to see that the five unicorns behind them were slowly gaining on them. Nova and Thunder were both carrying riders, and the other unicorns weren't. They were also younger and stronger in some ways. In moments, they would catch up to their targets.

Nova plunged on. Sweat was pouring down her flanks. It made Pixel's seating even harder, and his hands were getting sore from being locked so tightly into her mane. He kept waiting for one of their pursuers to reach them and impale him on his long, twisted horn. Pixel was panting furiously, and sweating even more than Nova, but this was mostly from fear.

And then they reached the stream that marked the boundary of the unicorn lands. Nova plunged in and surged across to the far bank. Thunder was just behind her. As they reached the bank, Nova tensed to run again, but Score cried: "No! Wait!"

Pixel glanced back, and saw Score had his chrysolite gem out, which gave him power over Water. Immediately, a sheet of water leaped into the air and froze solid, forming a wall of ice about four hundred feet long.

The five unicorns skittered to a halt, barely stopping in time to avoid hitting this frozen wall. They stared at it uncertainly, and then turned to go downstream and around it.

"I wouldn't try that if I were you," Score called out. "We're not on the herd lands any longer. This is *our* land, and we will stop you. We may not be able to work magic on you directly, but we can still work magic like that." He gestured at the ice wall.

The boy is right, Thunder agreed. *Go back to Tychus and tell him that we are gone. And tell him that I shall be back soon. Then he will have to fight me again — but fairly this time. Go!*

The unicorns might have pledged their loyalty to Tychus, but they were still used to obeying Thunder's orders. Besides, they could clearly see that further pursuit would be pointless. They turned back.

Pixel almost collapsed from relief. "That was close," he muttered, releasing his grip on Nova's mane and sliding to the ground. "I honestly didn't think we would make it."

Nor did I, agreed Nova, huffing and blowing. *I must be out of shape.*

You're in a lovely shape, Thunder assured her. He nuzzled her tenderly, and then yelled: *You! Off my back. The free ride's over.*

"Grouch," muttered Score as he dismounted. "Well, it's still early in the day. I guess you'll want to start out for the hidden valley now?"

Yes, agreed Thunder. *I am very eager to move on with this. We must find Darkstar and figure out what is happening.* He started off, Nova trotting with him. Pixel and Score brought up the rear.

"Great," groaned Score. "Another long hike. I *really* think we should think about getting bicycles or something in the future."

"It's an idea," agreed Pixel. "But I don't think we could do it magically."

"We don't have to," Score pointed out. "Now that we know how to open dimensional gates, we could just pop back to Earth and get some. Or anything else we wanted, for that matter."

"That's right," Pixel said. "It didn't even occur to me. You know, after this is over, we really ought to get together and decide if there's anything from other worlds we'd like to bring back to our castle."

"I can think of several," Score replied with a grin.

"But I don't think even McDonald's would want to open a franchise out here."

For a while they walked on in silence. Pixel considered what he'd like to bring here. The problem was that most of the stuff he was used to needed hooking up to a power grid, and there wasn't anything like that on Dondar. Unless, of course, he could figure out some way to operate his computer via magic instead of electricity. Well, it was something to think about at least! But Score's idea about bicycles was a good one. Though he had to grin at the thought of riding a bike while following a unicorn. It seemed rather silly.

After a while, Thunder called a halt. *We don't want the two of you getting tired out,* he said. *I've certainly had my fill of being ridden. And there are some nice fruit trees here, look.*

They gathered up plenty of the peculiar fruits of this planet and Pixel settled on a convenient rock to eat. "This Darkstar," he commented. "You say you and he were close. What was he like?"

Like? Thunder asked, puzzled. *Well, he was . . .* His thoughts trailed off, and he frowned. *That's odd. I can remember him quite clearly . . . except I can't remember anything *about* him.*

"You must be older than I thought," Score said, "if your memory's going like that."

It's not my memory, snapped Thunder. *It's just my memory of Darkstar.* He shook his head in confusion. *I can't even remember what he looked like.*

Pixel scowled. "That's not possible," he said. "You had a vision about him just a couple of hours ago. You *must* remember what he looked like."

No, Thunder answered. He sounded worried and scared. *Not a thing. I don't like this.*

It's not just Thunder, Nova added. *I can't remember anything about him, either. And I know I knew him very well.*

"Magic," Pixel said, with a dull feeling. "Somehow, you've both been affected by a spell that makes you forget all about Darkstar. It's the only explanation."

"And if it affects both of them," Score added, "I'll bet it affects the rest of the herd, too. For some reason, somebody doesn't want anyone to know about Darkstar. And that *somebody* has to be a magician."

Pixel sighed. "So we've got two problems here that may or may not be connected," Pixel summed up. "There's Tychus and this magician. They may be working together or separately. The key here is leadership of the herd, for some reason. Years ago, Darkstar was the leader, but he vanished for no known reason. And the unicorns have mostly forgotten about him because of a spell. Now Tychus has arrived and taken over the leadership using trickery — which could well have been supplied by this mysterious magician."

Well, can't you do something about it? asked Thunder. *The two of you are very powerful. Can't you take this spell off us?*

Pixel exchanged an unhappy look with Score. "I doubt it," he replied. "We may be *powerful*, but there's an awful lot we don't know. And I don't know any spells to counter forgetfulness. And even if we did, the memories may well be gone. All we could do is to stop you from losing any more. We can't restore what's lost."

I don't like the idea that someone's playing about with my mind, Thunder complained. *It's bad enough when my body's messed with, but now . . .* He shook his head. *I can't be sure which of my memories are real, or whether I've had others stripped from me, too. I feel like a house that's been robbed. It's a very disturbing feeling.*

"I can imagine," agreed Pixel. He threw away the core of the fruit he'd been eating, and washed off the stickiness in the small stream. "If you ask me, the best thing that we can do right now is to press on and find Darkstar before you forget about him completely."

"Forget about who?" asked Score innocently. Then he grinned and held up his hands. "Just kidding. Let's move on."

They traveled north for two more hours. The ground was starting to get quite rocky now, and in the distance loomed several mountains. Pixel eyed them unhappily.

"I hope we don't have to travel that far," he said. "They look rather rough, and we're not really equipped to climb any mountains."

"The problem with all of these cryptic messages," complained Score, "is that they're so vague about details. Like distances."

Just think yourself lucky that we didn't have to go through the dragon marshes, Thunder told them both. *Then you'd *really* have had something to complain about.*

Pixel eyed the sun. "Well, I guess we've got a few hours left before sunset. We'd probably better keep an eye open for a nice spot to camp out tonight." He sighed. "You know, I miss having Helaine along."

"Don't go all soppy on me," begged Score, rolling his eyes. "I don't think I could stand that."

"I didn't mean it *that* way," Pixel answered, unable to stop himself blushing. "I meant that it feels odd not having her. Besides which, she'd be able to hunt us up something for dinner. I'm getting tired of a fruit diet."

"Yeah, right," sneered Score. "That's all you

meant? Huh! Anyway, we don't need *her* to get us food. I'll do something."

"Sure you will," Pixel said sarcastically. "Snails or bugs, maybe. Nothing good."

Score shook his head, and produced one of the fruits. "You're forgetting my power to change things," he said cheerfully. He concentrated, and the fruit became a burger on a roll. "Or would you prefer to miss out on this?"

Pixel had forgotten about Score's skill for the moment. "Is that some of your Earth food?" he asked. "It looks interesting."

At that second, there came a terrible scream from the sky. Pixel looked up and swallowed in fear at what he saw. A huge shape was plummeting down at them, claws outstretched.

Pixel looked up and swallowed in fear at what he saw. A huge shape was plummeting down at them, claws outstretched.

Sphinx! screamed Nova, pure fear in her eyes as she reared back to face the attack.

CHAPTER 7

At the first scream from the air, Score had jerked out of his thoughts in shock and stared up at the source of the howl. At Nova's yell of *Sphinx*, he shuddered.

The creature was heading for them, ready to attack. Score had a brief glimpse of the creature. He had seen pictures of the stone Sphinx in Egypt in school once, but nothing could have prepared him for this.

It had the lower half of a lion, with huge claws extended to rip into flesh. It had the wings of an eagle, that must have been twenty feet from tip to tip, if they were spread instead of half-furled as they were now. The head was vaguely like a woman's, though her flowing hair was more like a lion's mane. Her eyes were yellow, and her teeth sharp and pointed like a cat's. A long tail flowed behind the creature, ending in a tuft of fur.

Move! yelled Thunder. Score didn't need a second warning. He shot for the safety of the nearest trees, knowing that would protect him from a dive. Pixel, too, bolted for cover.

But Nova didn't. She seemed to be frozen in fear, half-rearing, her horn upraised against the attack from the sky. Thunder hesitated a second, then rushed to his wife's aid.

He was almost too late. The Sphinx's wings suddenly spread wide to slow its plummet, claws extended to grip its prey. At the last second, it saw Thunder heading toward it, horn down to attack. The Sphinx beat its wings, trying to rise. As a result, its claws didn't sink into Nova's flesh, but instead left two lines of bright blood down her flank. Nova screamed in pain as the monster started to rise.

Thunder leaped, striking out with his horn as he did so. It sliced across one of the Sphinx's paws, and the creature gave a howl of pain as it rose in the air. But it wasn't retreating. Instead, it hovered in place a moment, warily watching Thunder.

He couldn't ignore it, but he nudged Nova gently. *To the trees,* he said firmly. *Now.* Shaking, she obeyed him, staggering as she moved. Thunder covered her retreat, watching the Sphinx the whole time.

Score couldn't work out what was going on. It wasn't like Nova to freeze up like that. And he didn't dare leave the safety of the trees to go and help her. The Sphinx was watching for any opportunity like that. He agonized as the two unicorns slowly made it back to safety.

"It can't get us in here," he said confidently, as Thunder and Nova joined them.

Don't be so sure of that, Thunder snapped. *In fact, it might even be easier for it. I can hardly charge at it in this confined space, can I?*

Score's confidence vanished. He stared at the creature, which appeared to have made up its mind. It flopped down to the earth, wincing as it touched its wounded paw to the ground. Like a cat, it lifted the paw to its mouth and licked at it for a moment. Then it folded its wings to its body and started toward the trees.

"I think it's time to panic," Score decided, eyeing the monster. It was almost twice the size of a lion, but with its wings tight against its body, it would have no problem at all in slipping through gaps in the trees. It was quite clearly a formidable creature.

"No," said Pixel firmly, though Score could see that he was shaking as he said it. "It's time for magic." He pulled the beryl from his pocket, which gave him control over the element of Air. "Nitrous oxide," he muttered.

Score had heard of that. "Laughing gas? You're planning on taking up dentistry?"

"Knockout gas," Pixel replied, focusing his thoughts.

It was a good idea. Score studied the Sphinx, hoping that Score's plan would work. If it got much closer . . .

The almost-human face looked confused, its nose wrinkling. And then it growled and raced forward.

"No good," Pixel gasped. "It has a great sense of smell, and detected the trap."

And now it was charging . . . Score's stomach churned, but he knew that the worst thing he could do in this situation would be to turn and run. It could leap on him and kill him instantly. Instead, he focused his thoughts and muttered the incantation to create a fireball. This was one trick he was getting down really well! Aiming, he threw the blazing ball at the Sphinx.

Which wasn't there anymore. It had leaped upward, out of the path of the missile. It was now almost on them.

"Scatter!" yelled Score, diving to one side.

The Sphinx almost had him. He could feel hot breath, and then the edge of one paw caught him, sending him reeling back into the bole of a tree. The blow stunned him for a second. He could do nothing but watch.

Pixel had reached cover and was scrambling to get a different gem to try another attack. But neither Nova nor Thunder had moved. Nova seemed to be in a trance, hardly aware of what was going on around her. Thunder had placed himself between her and the Sphinx, which had stopped when confronted with Thunder's horn.

Howling, the Sphinx reared up and lashed out with one huge forepaw. Thunder twisted his head to lance at it with his horn. The cat-thing yowled, and batted out with its other paw. Thunder managed to dance out of the way of the blow, but this couldn't go on for long.

Score's head was starting to clear. He took his emerald from his pocket and concentrated his thoughts on the ground where the Sphinx was standing. He had the power to change nonliving objects from one form to another with this gem, so he turned the ground beneath the Sphinx's feet into oxygen, opening a deep pit.

With a yelp of surprise, the Sphinx plunged downward.

"It won't hold it!" Pixel yelled. "It can just fly out again!"

"I know that!" Score snapped back. Using the

gem again, he then turned the air at the top of the hole into crystal, roofing the pit over. "That should stop it."

As he hurried forward, Score heard the Sphinx slam into the crystal, and the ground shook. "Uh, guys," he called. "That thing's *really* strong, and the pit won't hold it for long. We'd better retreat right now."

"I definitely second that motion," Pixel said. "Let's get in motion."

Nova made no attempt to move.

"What's with her?" Score yelled. "Come on, let's go — *now*, if not sooner."

She's afraid, Thunder answered. *It's shock.*

Score glanced down at the pit. He could see the Sphinx through the crystal he had created, leaping upward and slamming into the cover. There was already a faint crack in it. "Well, get her moving somehow," he snarled. "I don't care how. We can't stay here. That thing's too strong."

Pixel spotted a fallen branch, and picked it up. "Sorry, Nova," he muttered. Then he hit her across the flank, hard.

The blow got through to her. With a snort of pure fear, she suddenly took off like a rocket, fleeing deeper into the woods. Thunder huffed in surprise and then charged after her.

"Way to go," Score growled. "She's not going to stop before next week."

"At least she's moving!" Pixel answered. "And I really suggest that we do the same. Come on!"

Score needed no further urging. Tired as he had felt, he discovered that he had enough energy left to run for his life. The sounds of the Sphinx breaking free behind them diminished as they ran. Score concentrated on flight, watching for obstacles in his path, gasping for breath. After several minutes, he started to get a stitch in his side. He ignored it as best he could, hoping it would disappear. But it didn't. The pain became worse, and he had no option but to slow down and then collapse against the nearest tree.

Pixel flopped down beside him, panting and shaking. "I can't go on either," he admitted. "I'm still not used to this."

"Maybe we've come far enough," Score said wishfully, watching their back-path as he heaved for breath. The pounding of his heart was terribly loud, and his legs felt like jelly. "Anyway, at least Thunder and Nova got away."

"Yeah." Pixel looked around. "Maybe there's somewhere around here to hide," he suggested.

"Too late," Score replied, his insides quivering.

The Sphinx slid through the trees about twenty feet from them. Its yellow eyes burned with anger.

There were bloody streaks down its paws and across its flank that must have been caused by the crystal when it had broken free. Slowly, it stepped toward them.

Score leaned upright. There was no chance for them in running now. The Sphinx was really mad, and hardly even winded, while he and Pixel were totally exhausted. Magic would have to save them now. He formed another fireball, and hurled it at the creature.

It couldn't leap high out of the way this time because of the tree branches. But it did something Score hadn't expected. It reared up and used one of its paws to tug down a thick branch. The fireball slammed into this, setting it instantly ablaze, and the Sphinx simply let go of the branch. This then sprang back into the air, removing the fire from its path.

"That thing's too clever," Score muttered. As the Sphinx moved forward again, his fingers encompassed one of his gems. He looked down at it, frowning. It was the amethyst, a gem he'd never used before. What did it do? Oh, yes . . . It changed something's size . . .

And then he had it. Grinning in anticipation, he glowered back at the Sphinx. Like a cat, it was stalking him, certain of its prey. "Too clever," Score muttered, as he concentrated on the gemstone and the Sphinx. "And way too big for your boots."

The creature gave a squawk of fear as the magic enveloped it. It tried to run, but it was too late. The magic enfolded it, and Score watched in satisfaction as it seemed to compact in on itself, shrinking smaller and smaller.

He stopped when the Sphinx was only a foot long, and terrified. "You're not so ferocious now," he said. "More of a kitten than a lion. Boo!"

The tiny Sphinx turned and bolted. Score laughed out of sheer relief. Then he doused the fire that was still blazing in the tree before it set the whole forest alight.

"Well done," Pixel said approvingly. "That's certainly fixed it. The spell will wear off in a couple of hours, I'm sure, but I don't think it'll be back for more."

"I hope not," Score answered. "I don't think I'd want to face it again. Even with magic on our side, life isn't easy." He looked around. "Do you think we're still on the right track to catch up with Thunder and Nova?"

Pixel shrugged. "I guess we just head along and see," he replied. "I think I can manage a slow walk."

Together they set off, following the pathway. Score tried looking for unicorn tracks, but the pathway was used by a lot of animals, so he couldn't make out very much. Probably Helaine would have been able to, but not him.

Thinking of Helaine made him realize that Pixel had been correct earlier. It didn't feel right being here without her. Somehow, he'd gotten used to having her around. He was actually missing her, and that bothered him. He'd never been one to miss anybody before, and he didn't much like the feeling. This friendship business could really wreck your emotions.

Finally, after about an hour, they came to the banks of a narrow stream. "I think we'd better camp here," Score suggested. "It looks like it's going to be sunset pretty soon, and I'm famished."

Together, they built a small fire. Just as they were done with eating, there was a stirring in the trees. Score and Pixel jumped up, but then relaxed as Thunder and Nova emerged.

"Are we glad to see you both!" Score exclaimed. "Are you both okay?"

Almost, Thunder answered. He was leading Nova protectively. *But we're both very thirsty, and that water looks very inviting.* They both crossed to the stream and lapped for several minutes.

Score eyed them sympathetically. Running hard must have taken a lot out of them. They'd need a good rest tonight. "The Sphinx is gone," he told them. "I'm pretty sure we scared it off."

I'm sorry for my behavior, Nova answered, ashamed. *I was too panic-stricken to think clearly, and I endangered us all.*

"You couldn't help it," Pixel said kindly, stroking her neck. "We're all afraid of something."

When she was young, Thunder explained, *she and her mother were attacked by a Sphinx. Her mother pushed Nova to safety, but the Sphinx killed her mother and ate her. Nova's been terrified of the creatures ever since.*

"I can't blame you," Score said with a shudder. "That's horrible."

I'm fine now, Nova promised, though she seemed to be very subdued. *I'll be okay to go on in the morning. But I need rest right now.*

"We all do," Pixel said. "I'll take first watch for trouble. You guys get some sleep."

Score lay down, and was amazed at how quickly he fell asleep. He woke once, to take over his watch. It was a wonderfully clear night, with unfamiliar stars blazing in the sky. Two small moons hung near the horizon. It felt so weird and yet so lovely at the same time. Far different from New York City. After a few hours, he woke Thunder, and then fell asleep again.

It was sunlight when he woke again. Thunder was

still on watch, and he nickered a greeting. *Time for us all to get up,* he said. *It seems like a lovely day for travel.*

Despite the stiffness in his limbs, Score agreed.

"I hope it's not too far," Pixel grumbled. "I'm still sore from yesterday."

"You and me both," Score agreed. "But we're looking for a place of ice, don't forget." He waved his hands around. "I don't think it's going to be all that close."

He was completely wrong about that, though. It was only about two hours later when they reached a low range of hills. As they started to go between two of them, Thunder stopped, astonished.

Look at this! he exclaimed.

The two boys hurried to catch up with him. As they turned the curve in the road, they both stopped dead in their tracks.

The valley ahead of them was encrusted in ice and snow. A chill wind seeped from it, making them both shiver. Score turned to look behind them at the trees of summer, and then back at the depth of winter.

"This is crazy," he muttered. "It shouldn't be winter ahead and summer behind."

"It's not crazy," Pixel replied. "It's magic. I think that is what we were looking for. Darkstar must be in there somewhere."

CHAPTER 8

Helaine paced about the study in the castle impatiently. "So we know that there's a magician involved, but not who or why or where he is?"

Shrugging, Oracle replied: "For now. But I've been learning a few things that might help you. It's quite fun working with Shanara."

"I don't think you were exactly working with her," Helaine pointed out. "After all, you can't do magic, can you?"

"No, but I'm very supportive," he answered cheekily. "Anyway, this magician could hide his or her presence from Shanara because of the void between the worlds. It wouldn't necessarily stop *you* from locating the wizard."

Helaine hadn't thought of that. "But I don't know how to do that sort of thing. And I haven't seen any spell in my book that even refers to detecting magic. After all, it's usually pretty obvious when magic is being employed, so I guess nobody felt the need to point it out."

"Shanara knows how to do it," Oracle pointed out. "So with her help, you could manage, right?"

"But Shanara can't come to Dondar," Helaine answered, exasperated. "The power levels of the magic here would kill her. She's stuck on Rawn."

"You're thinking fuzzily again," Oracle told her. "It's a good job I'm around to set you straight. You can contact her using your agate."

Helaine blinked. "But she's on a different *planet*!" she exclaimed. "And on the Middle Circuit. Can it work over such a distance?"

"You're thinking in human terms again," Oracle told her with a sigh. "Magic isn't constrained the same way as shouting across a room is. You'll need to focus your power a little more than normal, but that shouldn't be too difficult. And Shanara is a magician, so she can help maintain contact."

Helaine shrugged. "Then let's see if you're right,"

she agreed. Gripping the agate, she concentrated on Shanara, and called out to her.

To her surprise, she could hear the magician's voice very clearly in her mind: *Helaine! So good to hear you again! Congratulations on defeating Sarman and the Triad.*

Thanks, Helaine replied. *Oracle told me that you discovered that there's a magician here messing things up. He seems to think that you can help me to detect him.*

Ow! said another voice, filled with sleep. *Shanara, that pinch *hurt*. I'm awake and paying attention.*

Stop moaning, Blink, and help out here, Shanara snapped. *Right, Helaine, you'll need some water in a bowl or basin of some sort. Can you manage that?*

No problem, Helaine answered. Getting a basin from Garonath's old supplies, she took it to the bathroom and half-filled it with water. *Now what?*

*Now you need to know a small spell. Blink, *wake up*! Now, tell Helaine what she needs to know.*

Botheration, muttered Blink. *Well, I suppose I'd better, otherwise I'll never get any peace, I can see. Helaine, pay attention and repeat this exactly.* He recited a short spell, which Helaine repeated back, word for word. *Good. Now, if you use your agate in conjunction with the water and that spell, it should reveal to you the position of the other magician. Now, I'm going back to sleep, so leave me alone.*

Silly thing, said Shanara. *Well, the spell should work, Helaine. Unless, of course, our magic-user is *very* powerful and can shield himself or herself against the spell. Good luck — and stay in touch, dear.*

The link was broken, and Helaine blinked as she came back to herself. "Well, I'm pretty sure I've got this down right," she said, standing over the bowl. She focused on the water through her agate and recited the spell: *Retlin zissu cha. . . .*

The water immediately turned slightly cloudy, and then a vague picture began to form. Helaine frowned down at it, urging it mentally to come into focus. Then she could see it getting clearer. There were trees, and horses . . . no, unicorns! And then it sprang into sharp focus and Helaine gasped.

It showed Tychus.

"Something's gone wrong," she said. "That's Tychus."

Oracle studied the bowl. "Well, you cast the spell properly, so he must be the magician."

"Oracle," Helaine growled, "he's a unicorn. Unicorns can't be magic-users. They can't manipulate magic because they *are* magical."

"Well, according to the spell, *he's* the one," Oracle argued. "So, either a unicorn *can* do magic, or else there's some other explanation. Maybe if you got close to him, you could find out for sure?"

"I probably could, except he's banished me from the herd." Helaine frowned and started pacing again. "He won't allow any human in again. And there's no point in sending you after him, because you couldn't tell if he was a magician or not."

Oracle grinned widely. "What you need," he told her, "is a disguise. If he won't allow a human in, maybe he'll allow something else in?"

Amazed, Helaine nodded and then grinned back. "My opal," she breathed, taking it from her pouch. "The power of transformation. I can magically make myself into something that is allowed in. Like a unicorn." A sudden thought came to her. "Hey! Maybe that's what Tychus has done! He could be a human magician who's assumed the shape of a unicorn."

"Now, that's a good thought," Oracle said approvingly. "If you can do it, I don't see why another magician couldn't. But doesn't such a transformation last only a short while?"

"A couple of hours at most," admitted Helaine. "Then you revert. But maybe he's got a way to stabilize the change? Or maybe he just goes off alone when he reverts and then waits till he can change back to reappear." She flicked through her Book of Magic. "Ah, I thought I remembered seeing this! It's a spell to cause someone to take on their true form again. *Fontecchio Simko zach.*" She quickly memorized it. "Now, if I can get to him and use this spell on him, if he *is* a changeling, I'll force him to change back. *That* should put a stop to all of his schemes. If the unicorns see him turn into a human, they're bound to expel him from the herd, and that will settle everything."

"It's certainly worth a try," agreed Oracle. "You know, the three of you constantly amaze me. You're very creative."

"Thanks." Helaine closed her book, and took out her opal. "Now it's time for you to go."

"What?" he asked. "And miss the interesting parts?"

"You can't go with me to the herd lands," she pointed out. "They would never allow you there."

Oracle sighed. "I'm not real, you know."

"You're too real for me," she snapped. "Go on, vanish. You can always come back later."

Oracle sighed and vanished. Helaine waited for a moment to be certain he wasn't going to simply pop back in again. Finally, she picked up the opal and concentrated on it, willing herself to become a unicorn.

There was a tingling throughout her body like nothing she had ever felt before. She could feel herself filled with power, and then the change began. The opal seemed to flow over her like a second skin, and she could feel her body altering. Her legs and arms started to elongate and thin out. Her neck stretched, and her face grew longer. Her hair contracted, and her back stooped down. There was a tail growing from the base of her spine, and her fingers and toes were fusing into cloven hooves.

Helaine dropped to all fours, and the world seemed to have changed totally around her. She was now a unicorn, and no longer a young woman. If she squinted, she could just see her horn, long, spiraled, and fascinating. She sniffed, her nostrils flaring, and she could smell everything in the room, her sense of scent a hundred times more powerful than it had been. She could feel an energy in her muscles like none she had ever known before. Her body was a light brown, flecked with a pale blue.

She moved slowly to the door, getting used to walking on four legs instead of two. Thankfully, she'd left it ajar, and she could nudge it open with her nose. She'd forgotten that in unicorn form she wouldn't have hands! She really should have done the transformation outside, but it had never occurred to her.

By the time she had left the castle and crossed the drawbridge, she felt a lot steadier on her feet. As her feet left the flagstones and touched the grass, she felt a lot better. She could smell a hundred different flowers and leaves that she had no names for in her weak human vocabulary. Her ears twitched, and she could hear the sound of the wind soughing through the branches of the trees. It felt glorious to be a unicorn!

Unable to control herself any longer, Helaine simply started to run down the path from the castle, toward the herd lands. Her mane and tail flew back as she ran, and she pounded the ground with an easy rhythm that was far faster and more elegant than walking or running as a human could ever be. She was almost sorry that this change couldn't last forever. She was starting to understand why unicorns had such a high opinion of themselves.

She ran on, happily enjoying the power and feel of this new body. She tapped through the stream that marked the boundary of the herd lands, and then ran on once more, toward the spot where the herd tended to congregate.

And then her path was blocked by another unicorn, this one a gleaming silver. *Halt!* he ordered. *Who are you? I have never seen you before.*

Uh-oh . . . Helaine stopped as she had been ordered. She realized that she couldn't use her agate with her for telepathy. It was transformed, like her clothes! For a second, she didn't know what to do. On the verge of panic, she realized that she was a unicorn. Maybe that included the power to *speak* like one. She could only hope . . . *I am Vixen,* she sent. *From a different herd.* "Vixen" was a name she had given one of her horses back on Ordin. Had this other unicorn heard her?

Oh, he replied. *I am Moondust. Why are you here?*

He *had* heard! So she was able to communicate. *I am related to one of your herd, Flame,* she replied. *I have come to visit with her.*

I see, he answered. *Well, proceed, then. But be wary. There may be humans about.*

Humans! Helaine sent a shudder through her thoughts. *I hope I don't meet any!*

Little chance of that, Moondust replied with a laugh. *But I am on guard duty here, otherwise I would escort you to Flame. You have nice fetlocks.*

Thank you, she replied coyly. *You're very handsome yourself.*

He preened at that, and then drifted back into hiding. Helaine continued on her way, thankful that she was past her first hurdle. It was quite a relief and a thrill at the same time. If she used her opal to transform herself into, say, a dragon, then presumably she'd actually be able to fly and spit fire.

That sounded like it could be fun.

Still, right now, she had a job to do. She trotted down the path toward the unicorn camp. Despite having run so much, she didn't feel the slightest bit tired. She could have kept going for hours. It was wonderful to feel so strong and alive. After a few minutes, she came to the main herd and stopped, puzzled.

They all seemed to be very subdued, which was definitely not normal for unicorns. They were always so full of life! What had happened? Helaine looked around for Flame, realizing, too, that there were no conversations being carried on. Again, that was very odd. Helaine was starting to get worried when she saw Flame off to her right. She slipped through the herd to reach her friend, puzzled that nobody challenged her or spoke to her. It was as if they were all sleepwalking or something.

Flame, she called as she drew near her friend. *Can you hear me?*

Flame raised her head slightly and looked back at Helaine, but there was neither recognition nor curiosity in her eyes. Helaine hadn't expected to be recognized in this guise, of course, but Flame was normally very inquisitive. What had happened to her?

Flame, she said, standing right next to the gold-flecked unicorn. *It's me. Helaine.*

Helaine? repeated Flame, sounding confused.

Helaine, she repeated. *I'm disguised as a unicorn and —*

Suddenly, Flame jerked to life. *Human!* she screamed. *There's a human among us!*

Confused, Helaine took a step back. *What?* she exclaimed. Her friend had deliberately betrayed her to the rest of the herd! Helaine couldn't believe it.

Human! Flame howled again, and then tossed her head. *I shall fight her!* And she lowered her horn to charge.

Flame, don't do it! Helaine cried. *I don't want to fight you. You're my friend.*

You're a human! Flame stated. *And I don't make friends with humans.* Then she charged.

Helaine sidestepped the attack, but she didn't know what to do. She didn't want to hurt Flame, and she couldn't understand why she was acting like this. The rest of the herd had started to waken and surround them, and Helaine knew she'd not be able to get out of here again. What was happening to the unicorns?

Whirling, Flame charged again. Once more, Helaine dodged aside, but she felt the wind as Flame's horn almost gashed her side. If she didn't defend herself, Flame might do some serious damage next time. *Flame!* she cried. *Please stop fighting me! I'm your friend!*

Liar! Flame yelled back and whirled to charge again.

Stop! came a powerful voice. Tychus stepped from the crowd, studying the scene with interest. *So, we have an intruder.*

Yes, Flame answered. She was now standing still as ordered. *It is the human known as Helaine, disguised as a unicorn.*

Oh. Tychus stepped forward. *Quite a clever little plan,* he admitted. *But my unicorns will not tolerate any humans.*

What have you done to them? demanded Helaine, furiously. She could see no way of escaping the encircling unicorns.

I have awakened them to the true state of affairs, Tychus replied. *Now, I think the best thing to do here is to return you to your true shape.* He stepped back, and then called out: *Enclose her with your horns, and strip the magic from her.*

Helaine couldn't allow that to happen, because her only means of defense right now was magic. Instead, she recited the spell to restore her to her human shape. *Fontecchio Simko zach.* It happened swiftly, and she felt a pang of regret as she lost her unicorn form and became human again.

Then she immediately unleashed the changeling spell onto Tychus, willing him to revert to his true form. She might have been exposed, but he would he be as well!

Fontecchio Simko zach!

Nothing happened.

Helaine stood there in shock for a moment, staring at Tychus. Nothing had changed . . . which meant that he wasn't a magician simply masquerading as a unicorn. Her theory had been wrong!

Laughing, Tychus shook his head. *So *that* was your plan? To try and expose me as a false unicorn? My dear, you have far more courage than you have brains. I *am* a true unicorn, but one such as you've never known.* To the other unicorns, he called: *Encircle her and drain her power before she uses it against you!*

As the herd started to close in on her, Tychus stood outside the circle, watching. Helaine was worried. She had to do something *now*. She had to transform herself into something which could escape. Something that could fly — except that she didn't know how to fly, and learning would take some time. Something large and powerful then, that the unicorns wouldn't dare attack. She began to concentrate on changing into a fire-breathing dragon. But she was tired from the earlier change, and the unicorns closed in on her faster than she had expected. She couldn't summon the power to change!

And then she was enveloped in glowing unicorn horns. She could feel her magical abilities being drained from her. It was only temporary, of course, but the effect would last for several hours. Until her power came back, she was just a lone human surrounded by the herd.

Tychus called: *Enough!* and the unicorns ceased their draining. *She's completely depleted and harmless now,* he said. He moved forward, the herd falling back to allow him passage. *You are my captive now,* he informed Helaine. *You were warned what would happen if you attempted to return. In a short while, you will die.*

CHAPTER 9

Pixel stared at the ice-clad valley in front of them. "That has to be the place that Darkstar meant," he said. "It's too weird to be anything else."

"And there's something on that rock over there," Score pointed out. It was a flat-topped rock by the entrance to the valley, and Pixel could see that something had been carved into the top of it. They hurried over to examine it.

"Cdraagveon?" Score asked. "Does that mean anything to anyone here? Because it sure isn't ringing any of my bells."

Pixel nodded, as if he hadn't heard Score. Everyone fell silent, awaiting his solution.

"It's actually an old word game," Pixel explained. "The word *dragon* is inside the word *cave.* Which means there's a cave around here somewhere . . . with a dragon inside."

And the next phrase? Thunder asked.

The same thing, Nova answered, catching on to Pixel's logic. *There are prisoners inside the ice inside the cave.*

"Exactly," Pixel agreed.

So we must find our way to the ice cave . . . which is guarded by a dragon, Thunder stated.

"A dragon?" Score shook his head. "That's got to be crazy. Dragons are flying things that spit fire."

Not always, Thunder replied. *There are many sorts of dragons. Some walk on the ground, and many can't breath fire. Some hoard gold, and others live in wells or under the sea.* He shrugged. *Perhaps there is a dragon living here that enjoys the cold.*

"Well, I don't very much," Score complained. "And I'm not really dressed for winter sports. So if we've got to go in there, let's do it as fast as possible and then beat a hasty retreat to somewhere warm and sunny. Disney World would be my first choice."

I've never heard of that planet, Nova answered. *Is it nice?*

Score grinned. "Maybe I'll take you there one day." He scavenged around for a couple of fallen branches, and handed one to Pixel. Realizing what he had in mind, Pixel conjured up fire at the end, so they both had torches that provided a little warmth.

"Okay," Pixel said. "We'd better start looking for that cave." He led the way forward, his feet crunching in the snow.

Behind him, he could feel Nova shiver. *Ugh!* she muttered. *I hate the cold. It's freezing my hooves.*

He turned and patted her gently on the nose, and she nuzzled him. There wasn't much that they could say. He led the way into the valley, and they gradually left all hints of summer behind them. It was like the time he'd walked through a glacier in Virtual Reality, except, of course, that it was *cold* here. Even with the torch he carried, he could feel the chill creeping into his bones. If they were here for too long, they would freeze to death.

But how far did they have to go?

He crunched his way on through the snow, staring

up at the sun. It looked full and bright, but none of its heat seemed to be penetrating here. And then he caught a glimpse of a jagged blackness in the side of the iced hill.

"There's the cave!" he exclaimed happily. "We're halfway there now. I hope."

They moved on a little faster now that their destination was in sight, and reached it in about ten minutes. It had to be what they were looking for, and it was larger than he'd expected. The entrance was about ten feet around and went back as far as the light from their torches could reach. The walls were all covered with ice, and the floor with packed snow. It would be difficult to walk on, but not impossible.

"I was hoping it would be a small cave," Pixel confessed. "But it looks like it goes in quite deep."

Then we had better follow it, said Thunder, *before my hooves freeze off.*

Nodding, Pixel again led the way. The flames from his and Score's torches glittered wildly in the ice on the walls, creating an almost searchlight-like effect as they walked. But it was no warmer in the cave than outside, and Pixel's feet were starting to feel the chill even through the insulated soles of his sneakers. There was only so much of this that they could all endure.

After about forty feet, sloping downward, they were presented with a real problem. The cave split into two passageways.

"Now what?" asked Pixel. "Which do we take?"

I have no idea, Thunder replied. *The clues Darkstar left didn't mention two passages. Either one could be the right one.*

Then we'll have to split up, Nova said practically. *You and Score take the left-hand tunnel, and we'll take the right. If either of them comes to an end, then we'll just retrace our steps and take the other tunnel.*

"And if these tunnels also split?" asked Score.

Thunder and I can use our horns to mark the path we're taking, Nova replied. *That way, we can track one another.*

Pixel sighed. "I don't like splitting up," he admitted, "but it seems like the best thing to do right now." He gave Score a shaky smile. "Good luck."

"Yeah, you too." Score swallowed and started down his tunnel. Thunder nuzzled Nova affectionately, and then followed.

"Right," Pixel said, leading the way into the right-hand tunnel. It continued to lead gently downward, and he realized that they had to be below ground level by now. How far down would the tunnel eventually lead them? And would they be able to walk all the way back out again without freezing? And what about the dragon that the clue had mentioned. He couldn't see how one could possibly live down here without freezing to death. Maybe it meant a dead dragon? He certainly hoped so! It would be much better than finding a live one at the end of their path . . .

Nervously, he walked ahead, scanning for anything. The passageway opened out to about fifteen feet across, and he felt a little more confident.

Then there was a loud *crack!* from beneath his feet. The ground gave way.

With a cry of shock, Pixel started to fall, dropping his torch. It immediately fizzled out in the snow, leaving him falling in blackness. There was some sort of pit that had only been covered by a thin layer of ice and snow, and his weight had been too much for it! Before he could fall through the gap in the ice, though, he felt Nova's teeth grip the sleeve of his shirt, and he jerked to a halt, heart pounding wildly.

Grab hold of my neck, she commanded. *I can't hold on to this cloth for very long.*

Pixel managed to swivel about and grasped hold of her neck with his free hand. She released her grip with her teeth, and then slowly pulled him from the pit. A moment later, he had solid ground beneath his feet again. He stood there, shaking with shock. "Thanks," he gasped. "I thought I was doomed."

The ground here is as treacherous as it is cold, she replied. *We had better proceed with more caution.*

"I agree." Pixel managed to retrieve his torch from where it had fallen and relit it. He could see the pit now. There was no bottom to it in sight. He shuddered again. "We should stick close to the walls," he decided. "There's less likely to be pits there. And I'll stay in the lead. You might be able to pull me to safety, but there's no way I could do the same for you, I'm afraid."

I understand.

They set off again. Pixel was nervous and uncertain about each step he took, but the floor seemed to be more solid closer to the walls, as he had hoped. After a while, his heart settled back to its normal pace again, and the sick taste of fear evaporated from his mouth.

They had been traveling for about fifteen minutes when something puzzled him. "Look at this," he said, gesturing to the ice covering the wall. It wasn't perfectly clear, of course, more a sort of milky color. You couldn't see the underlying rocks or anything. But at this point in the wall, there was some kind of a shadow in the ice. It was about four feet tall, and a couple of feet wide. "What do you make of that?"

Some defect in the ice, I imagine, Nova answered. *Is it at all important? If not, we should press on.*

"I agree." It was hard not to shiver as he moved now. Pixel was afraid his teeth were going to start chattering. Then, about twenty yards further on, there was another shadow in the ice, this one larger and wider. And another about thirty yards later. Pixel couldn't help wondering what this meant. Were these just spots that had less ice than others, allowing the rocks beneath to show through? Or was there some other reason for the shadows?

Finally, having passed two more, he could stand the curiosity no longer. He halted, and turned to Nova. "It's no use," he said. "I'm certain there's some significance to these shadows, and I've got to know what it is."

You young humans are curious about everything, Nova replied with a sigh. *Personally, I'd sooner press on, but I can see I'd better humor you about this. Try to be fast, *please*."

Pixel nodded. Then he concentrated on creating a very hot fireball, and launched it at the wall of ice.

The fireball didn't last very long, sizzling out in a shower of water, but it melted a hole about two feet across and four deep into the ice. Deep enough to reveal what the shadow was.

It's a griffin, Nova exclaimed in astonishment.

Pixel nodded, staring through the few inches of ice remaining over it. He could see the hawk-like face of the creature embedded in the wall, and part of the line of one claw. Its eyes were open, but it quite clearly wasn't alive.

"This must be what Darkstar meant," Pixel realized. "When he told Thunder in that vision that he'd been sleeping for years, and wished that he were dead. I'll bet he's entombed somewhere in here, frozen solid. Neither dead nor alive."

Nova nodded. *But . . . there are so many shadows. Which one of them is Darkstar? We could hunt for years and never know.*

Taking his ruby from his pocket, Pixel grinned. "Now that I know what to search for, I can try a little magic," he replied. "When I last tried this, I was looking for a living unicorn. That's why I found nothing. Now I know I have to look for a frozen one." He concentrated, and a beam of rich redness flashed along the path ahead of them. Pixel concentrated on the image he could see. "He's in a chamber not far ahead," he told Nova. "In the wall of ice there. He's very close to death, but still alive for the moment."

Then let us go after him, Nova replied urgently.

Pixel nodded, and led the way. He knew from his magic that there wasn't far to go. It took them about five minutes to reach the chamber, and they halted in the entrance.

The chamber was several hundred feet across. As well as ice lining the walls, icy stalactites hung from the roof. Dozens of crystalline stalagmites grew upward from the ground. There were mounds of ice and snow all around. In the tiny light from Pixel's torch, the cavern gleamed like a treasure chamber filled with jewels.

"He's over here," Pixel said, whispering without knowing why. This place was awesome, like some immense cathedral carved from living ice. He moved to a section of the wall about twenty feet from the doorway. There was a large shadow inside the ice. "All we have to do is free him now."

Then he heard a soft hissing noise, like a steam engine or a kettle. Puzzled, he looked around the cave, but saw nothing. He gazed uneasily at Nova, whose nostrils flared suddenly.

There is something here that is very much alive, she told him. *But it is something I have never encountered before.*

"I'm getting a really bad feeling about this," Pixel muttered. But he could see nothing.

And then he realized that one of the piles of ice and snow was moving slightly, as if something under it were cracking free of its frozen prison. "Look!" he said, pointing.

And then he realized that he had been mistaken. The ice wasn't *breaking*, it was moving. It was somehow alive . . . As he watched in amazement, the ice pile suddenly resolved itself by movement. He could see it was actually a living creature, with its body formed of blocks like ice. There was a long body and tail, about twenty feet in length. Four massive legs, and a large head on a sinuous neck. Two eyes, pale blue specks in icy depths, stared down at them, and a fierce mouth opened.

"A dragon," he gasped, now understanding what the clue had meant.

*An *ice* dragon,* Nova added. *Instead of fire, this one breathes —*

A blast of absolute cold hit them both, coating them in a layer of ice. Pixel was instantly frozen inside a block of thick ice, Nova close beside him. He could feel his life starting to ebb away, and realized that, far from rescuing Darkstar, he and Nova had become trapped inside the ice themselves.

In moments, they, too, would be frozen corpses in the ice dragon's collection . . .

CHAPTER 10

Score was getting colder and colder as he and Thunder walked in silence through the ice corridors. He remembered being on the streets in New York one winter when a foot of snow had fallen and he was hiding out from his father. He'd thought he was going to freeze to death then. And that felt like a summer day compared to being in this cave.

Having to backtrack and take the other tunnel hadn't improved either his or Thunder's moods, either. After fifteen minutes of travel, the left tunnel had come to an abrupt end. Miserably, they had started back and set off after Pixel and Nova. They were both too cold to even argue with one another.

They had to skirt a hole in the ice at one point. Score had been momentarily afraid that either Pixel or Nova had fallen through, until he had seen their footprints in the snow continuing along the side wall. Relief washed over him: losing either of their companions would have been a devastating blow.

Then, later, they had seen the shadows in the ice and finally come across the hole melted through to the griffin. Both of them had realized the significance of this.

"Something's freezing intruders into the ice," Score said. "And whatever it is must be up ahead."

And Nova and Pixel are going to confront it first, growled Thunder. *I think we'd better move faster and catch up with them.*

"If we can," gasped Score. He felt as if he were a barely moving lump of ice already. But he managed to speed up a little. Thunder was still having problems walking on the snow. He wasn't complaining for once, but Score could tell that the cold was really hurting his feet.

Then they came to the cavern and immediately saw the light from Pixel's torch. They were also just in time to see the ice dragon rear up and eject a cloud of frost at Pixel and Nova, who were instantly frozen inside a block of ice.

"No!" howled Score in despair. He'd only just

learned how to make friends, and he wasn't going to lose any now. Hastily, he created the largest fireball he could manage and threw it with all of his might at the block containing Pixel and Nova, exploding it just before it hit.

Instantly, the ice melted, running in streams off the trapped pair. To Score's relief, both shook themselves, shivering from the cold and the closeness of their escape.

Then Thunder shoved Score aside as the ice dragon coiled around and breathed in their direction. A wave of frigid air narrowly missed embracing them both as Thunder leaped aside, too. They ducked for cover behind the resulting iceberg-shaped formation.

"It can't move very fast," gasped Score. "It's cold-blooded, literally. So we could run rings around it if we were in the open."

But we're too cold to run in here, pointed out Thunder. *And it's fast enough to get us if we leave cover.* Then he ignored Score and called: *Nova!*

We're all right, came her answer. *We're hiding behind a stalagmite. That was *very* close, though.*

Stay there, Thunder ordered. He glared down at Score. *She may say that they're all right, but they narrowly escaped death. I think we should not count on them too much for what may happen next. I sincerely hope you have *some* idea of how to defeat that creature?*

"Why do you expect *me* to come up with something?" complained Score. "I thought humans were useless?" He shook his head. "Maybe a well-placed fireball might melt that dragon's heart . . ." Forming the last one had drained his strength, but he managed to make one of a respectable size. Stepping out from behind cover, he threw it at the dragon's head, which was already questing for them.

Another icy blast came from the huge mouth, enveloping and extinguishing the fireball. Score ducked back into cover.

"Scratch that idea," he grunted. "And we can't get close to it. Its body temperature is so low that anything it touches turns instantly to ice, so we can't physically attack it. Your horn would just turn brittle and break. So what we need is a brilliant idea."

And I'm relying on you to come up with one, Thunder answered. *I *really* must be losing my mind.*

"You've not lost it," Score informed him. "You never had it to begin with." Then a sudden thought occurred to him. "*Anything it touches turns instantly to ice* . . ." he breathed. "That's the answer! Now I know how to beat it."

Then stop talking and do it!

Score shook his head and sighed. He took out the chrysolite. This gave him power over Water, and ice was just frozen water, after all . . . The dragon froze its victims inside blocks of ice, so he had an idea for an appropriate way to defeat it.

He took a quick peek to confirm that the dragon was about twenty feet closer to him, and then focused on the ice on the ceiling above it. He radiated warmth throughout it, melting the ice into a gigantic torrent of water that cascaded down.

All over the dragon.

As it touched the dragon's frozen skin, the water instantly became ice. Layer after layer of it built up in seconds, as more water touched and became frigid. In moments, before the dragon could react, it was buried inside several feet of ice that held it solidly in place.

Score stepped out of hiding and grinned happily as he surveyed his handiwork. The dragon was caught inside a huge block of ice, as frozen as any of its victims. "Well," he said, smugly, "I think that was pretty brilliant. You can applaud if you like."

Thankfully, Thunder snapped back, *I don't have hands and therefore couldn't even be tempted to do so.* He hurried as fast as he could over the ice to rejoin and nuzzle his wife. Score, grinning widely, followed him. "How are you doing?" he asked Pixel.

"Chilled to the bone," the other boy admitted. "But still alive, thanks to you."

"Hang on," Score said. Using his gem, he evaporated the water from Pixel's clothes, which should at least prevent him from hypothermia. "Maybe we should try and go somewhere warm for a while," he suggested.

"There's no time for that," Pixel answered. He gestured to a shadow inside the ice beside them. "This is Darkstar. It's why we couldn't find him earlier. He's been trapped."

"Then I guess we'd better set him free," said Score. "You think he's still alive inside there?"

He must be, Thunder insisted. *He managed to project his mind to me. So he must still be alive.*

"Right," said Pixel, grimly. He conjured up a fireball, and used it to melt the ice. It was slow going, because he had to be sure not to injure the trapped unicorn. When Score's strength came back, he helped, too. Handling the fires warmed them both up, which was a pleasant side-effect of the business, but Score still couldn't wait until they could beat a hasty retreat from this place.

Finally, Darkstar was free. He took a deep, shuddering breath and collapsed to the ground. *Thank you,* he managed to send. *You have freed me at last. Now, you must listen to me. There is not much time.*

We can get you out of here, to a warm place, Thunder said urgently. *Then you'll be fine.*

No, Darkstar told him. *I was dying anyway before that ice dragon trapped me. I've been magically poisoned, and have only a short time left. His freezing me ironically saved me from dying by the poison. But now I am free, the poison is acting again. So listen to me. What I have to tell you is vitally important.

Your foe is the magician Marmanki. He and Sarman grew up together. Sarman aims to take control of the entire Diadem.

"Relax," Score told him. "We've already beaten Sarman. The guy's history."

Ah! Then that explains it! Darkstar nodded slightly. Any movement was clearly hard for him. *The two of them were friends, but Sarman's passion for power made him suspicious even of his friend and he killed Marmanki.*

"Then how can he be our foe?" asked Score, puzzled.

Because Marmanki has come up with a new form of magic, explained Darkstar. *When he is killed, he has the power to move his life-force and take possession of the body nearest to his at the time. So he escaped from Sarman in the guise of a bird and then transferred to a new body later. What Marmanki then plotted was to gain protection for himself. He wanted unicorn horns so that he could guard himself against further magical attacks. And also to sell and trade with other magicians who could use them. So he planned on taking over our herd.

*I know all of this because I was the leader when he struck. He came in the guise of another unicorn, planning to kill me and take control of the herd. I was too strong for him, though, and killed him. But he did not stay dead, transferring into the closest creature to him. He had expected it to be me, so that in my guise he could take over the herd, but fate betrayed him.

We had been fighting directly above the nest of a basilisk.

"A what?" asked Score.

A magical creature that has a stare that will poison you incurably. It also sleeps for years at a time, crawling out only from time to time to feed. Marmanki wakened in its body and then gave me the magical stare. That is what is killing me. He then planned to kill the basilisk and take over another unicorn. What he hadn't counted upon was that the basilisk was still in need of hibernation, and so he fell asleep again for several years.

"Only to wake up a short while ago and transfer into Tychus's body," Pixel exclaimed. "And with Sarman out of the way, he can now carry on with his old plan of taking over the unicorn herd and killing them for their horns."

Exactly, agreed Darkstar. *I was delirious from the poison, and wandered away from the herd. I managed to carve a message to you showing where I was going, Thunder, so that you would know what had happened to me. I stumbled into the ice cave here, coming to die, when the dragon attacked and froze me. I dreamed the years away, longing to be free in death. Then I felt your mind and managed to send you my message for you to come here.*

Too late to save you, Thunder said sadly.

But you freed me, Darkstar answered. *And I am able to tell you my story so that you will be able to return to save your herd from Marmanki's plans. You must hurry back to them and rescue them now. Marmanki plans to kill them all and then restore himself to human form.*

We will return, promised Thunder. *He shall not kill those under my protection.*

You are a good leader, Thunder, Darkstar said approvingly. *Better, I know, than I ever was.* Then he gave a sigh, and lay still.

"He's . . . dead," Pixel said quietly.

Thunder knelt down by the body, his head bowed. *No,* he said gently. *No one could be better than you. But I shall do my best.*

Something unsettling had occurred to Score. “Come on, guys,” he complained. “I know you’re broken up, but we don’t have the time for this. We have to get back to the herd immediately.”

Why the urgency? asked Nova. *Marmanki won’t do anything to the unicorns until he has a human body he can transfer into.*

“And he’s *got* one,” Score snapped. “Don’t forget that *Helaine* is keeping an eye on the herd. If she’s anywhere close to Tychus, and the unicorn kills himself . . . then he’s got himself a new body. Hers.”

CHAPTER 11

Helaine considered the story she'd just heard from Tychus. "So you spent the past five years asleep as a basilisk?" she summed up. "And then started your plan up again?"

Correct, agreed Tychus. *And I am now exactly where I had hoped to be. The herd was very careless, convinced that no magic could affect them. But I have worked it from within. I cast a spell five years ago for them all to forget about Darkstar, which seems to have held up well. I have now done the same to them all for Thunder and you humans. The herd is in my power, and they will all obligingly allow me to kill them and remove their horns. And since you and your friends have killed Sarman for me, I shall be the most powerful magician in the whole Diadem.*

"You're disgusting," Helaine said. She stared at him in puzzlement. "It was very nice of you to let me keep my sword. After all, my power is still drained and I couldn't do it myself. But what's in it for you?"

Do you think I intend to remain as a unicorn forever? asked Tychus — or, rather, Marmanki, which was his real name. *I'd be prey to anyone who desired a unicorn horn. No, I want a *real* body again. A human body. And yours will do very nicely. Oh, I know it's female, but it's definitely a step up from being an animal.*

"Unicorns aren't animals," Helaine replied. "You should know that." She felt sick at hearing his plans — not just those concerning her, but concerning the herd. "How can you just plan to kill them all?"

Because of the power it will bring me, he answered. *No other magician will be able to harm me, and only those who ally themselves with me will be given a horn of their own. You three pathetic children may not value power, but I'm not as stupid as you.*

"You don't have a conscience at all, do you?" Helaine asked.

"Consciences are for those without power."

She shook her head. This was a common attitude among magic-users. They thought they were better than everyone else, and so above all normal laws and rules. Selfish, through and through. "I won't let you get away with it," she warned him.

Fine, he replied with a laugh. *I've given you your sword back. Let's see how you can do in a fight with a unicorn. I'm not entirely without a sense of honor. I aim to kill you, but I'm giving you a chance to fight back. Not that you can win, of course. You're just a *girl*.*

Those were fighting words to Helaine. All her life, she'd been scorned and considered a very second-class citizen simply because she had been born a girl in a world where only boys got to have any say in matters, or to have any fun. It was why she'd disguised herself as a boy and adopted the alias of Renald. And here was this murderous magician taunting her about being a girl! She drew her sword and stood on the plain, waiting.

Marmanki laughed again, lowered his horn, and charged.

At the last moment, Helaine moved aside, whipped her sword around, and parried the thrust of the horn. Marmanki laughed and danced away.

A poor effort, he jeered. *Is that the best you can do?*

"Try me, and you'll see," she offered, standing ready for the next pass. He lowered his horn, moved into position, and then charged. This time, Helaine moved in the opposite direction, whirling around to strike at Marmanki's throat. The unicorn wasn't quite quick enough to dodge her, and she had a clear, killing blow.

She managed to stop the strike at the very last second, allowing the sword to tumble from her fingers.

Marmanki stood there, blood trickling from the cut she had inflicted, and laughed at her. *Coward!* he spat. *For all your boasting, you're no warrior. You're a pathetic weakling.*

"No," Helaine answered, shaking as she realized how close she'd come to dying by being so foolish. "You're trying to provoke me into attacking you, but it won't work. I just realized what you were trying to do. You're not trying to kill *me*! You want my body. You're trying to get *me* to kill *you*! That way, you can transfer out of that body and into the nearest one. *Mine*. You almost suckered me into getting myself killed, didn't you? But it won't work now. I won't fight you."

The unicorn eyed her with fresh respect. *You're not quite as stupid as you appear to be, are you?* He laughed. *Yes, that was what I was attempting to do. It almost worked, too. But there are other ways to accomplish the same end. You haven't beaten me yet.* He turned away from her, staring across the field.

A moment later, Flame came trotting across the field. He'd obviously summoned her telepathically. Unsure of what he was planning, Helaine picked up her sword, cleaned it, and then resheathed it. She wouldn't use it on him, but she wanted it close by in case of trouble.

Marmanki turned to her with a nasty smile. *Your good friend Flame is under my mental domination, and she'll do anything I tell her to do. And now I order her to *kill me.**

Helaine gasped in shock as Flame suddenly started forward, her horn down in the attack position, hurtling straight toward the waiting Marmanki. With a cry, Helaine tried to intervene. But she couldn't get there in time . . .

At the last second, Flame turned her horn aside and narrowly missed Marmanki. Helaine sighed in relief. It had to have been some kind of a trick of his to fool her! Then she realized that she'd jumped to the wrong conclusion.

Idiot! Marmanki screamed. *Weakling!* He glared at Flame, who was standing with her head bowed, and then at Helaine. *She's as stupid as you. Even in her current state, she won't kill a helpless foe.*

"Give it up, Marmanki," Helaine sneered. "She's

got too much moral courage for you to subvert. She's not going to do your dirty work for you."

Oh, no, Marmanki replied. *There's more than one way to kill a unicorn.* He stared at Flame, who gave a shudder. *Your mind is your own again. Your memories are your own again. Only Helaine is in my control now, and I'm going to kill her. You can't stop me!* He whirled and launched himself at Helaine.

Helaine! screamed Flame. *No!* And she threw herself into the pursuit.

Marmanki, of course, deliberately missed Helaine by inches. He had no desire to harm the body he hoped to possess. Helaine had stood calmly, awaiting him, knowing he wouldn't even bruise her. But Flame mistook the reason.

*Helaine, *run*!* she yelled. *I'll stop him.*

"No, Flame!" Helaine cried. "He won't hurt me."

*He's just making you *believe* that,* Flame answered. *You're under his mental control. Fight it and flee.* Then she whirled about to charge at Marmanki again.

This time, Helaine knew, she wouldn't hesitate to kill. She was sure that "Tychus" was going to kill her best friend, and she'd kill for Helaine.

Not knowing, of course, that this was exactly what Marmanki wanted.

Helaine did the only thing she could think of.

She threw herself directly in the path of Flame.

For a second, all she could see was the unicorn horn, pointed straight at her chest. She knew that it was going to ram into her and kill her instantly. Flame was traveling too fast to avoid the killing blow now. Helaine felt fear, and despair, and a terrible knowledge that Flame would blame herself for the deed.

And then the horn moved slightly, as Flame managed to twist herself out of direct collision somehow. Instead, the horn sliced across Helaine's left bicep, drawing blood and pain, and then Flame's shoulder slammed into Helaine. The blow threw Helaine from her feet, and tumbled her to the ground, groaning.

For a moment, Helaine felt nothing but pain all over.

And then she heard Marmanki in her mind yell: *You *idiot*! If you've harmed her body, I'll *kill* you!*

Then came Flame's stunned response: *Helaine was right. You *aren't* trying to kill her.*

Helaine groaned again, but managed to raise herself on her right arm. Blood was dripping from her left, and she could hardly move it. "Listen to me, Flame," she gasped, through a red haze. "Don't harm him. He can transfer to a new body — the closest body — if he's killed and he wants mine."

So that's it. Flame trotted back to stand beside Helaine. *Then I shall have to make certain that he stays alive. I'm sorry for what I did to you, Helaine.*

"It was my fault. I just couldn't think of any other way to stop you in time." Helaine winced as she managed to sit up. "I'm going to be bruised all over, I know it." She held her right hand over her bleeding arm. "And one-handed, too. But I'm glad I'm still alive. I was certain you couldn't avoid killing me. And I'm really glad you did."

This doesn't mean anything, Marmanki cried angrily. *There are other unicorns in the herd. One of them will kill me.*

Ah, but it'll do you no good at all if Helaine's not the closest thing to you when you die, will it? Flame asked. She looked down at her friend. *Can you get up, Helaine? We have to escape from here.*

No! Marmanki thundered. *Perhaps I can't harm *her*, but I'm under no such constraints with *you*.* He lowered his horn and started toward Flame.

But Marmanki's luck had run out. Taking his time to explain his actions to Helaine and the subsequent fighting had taken far longer than he'd anticipated. Helaine could feel her power returning now. Not a lot of it, true, but enough so that she could do some simple magic, aided by her crystals. Clutching at her chrysoprase tightly, she concentrated on the ground in front of Marmanki.

The ground beneath his feet started to quiver and shake. Marmanki lost his footing and stumbled. He glared furiously at Helaine. *These tricks won't stop me!* he promised her. *You can't defeat me.*

"Give it up, Marmanki," Helaine begged him. "Now we know your powers, you can't possibly win against us."

You can't stop me from dying, Marmanki replied. *And then I'll be back, in some other guise. You can't check every last creature or insect that enters the unicorn lands from now on. And you'll never know if one of them might be me.*

Helaine realized with a sinking feeling that he was absolutely right. They couldn't kill Marmanki, and they didn't dare leave him alive. There didn't seem to be any solution to this nightmare. Marmanki smirked, realizing that he now had the advantage again.

I'm invincible, he assured her. *My power makes me so. There is *nothing* that you can do to stop me.*

"Boy," said a very familiar voice, "he's really arrogant, isn't he?"

Helaine whirled around, to see Score and Pixel grinning at her. They both looked very tired, though. Pixel didn't even seem to have the energy to talk.

"Teleportation," Score told her. "Takes it out of

you, though. We hurried back to warn you about Marmanki, but it looks like you've already figured it out."

Helaine clutched her agate, and sent a reply to her friends telepathically. *Am I glad to see the two of you! But where are Thunder and Nova? What happened?*

Later, Score answered. *The problem right now is Marmanki.*

You're telling me? she replied dryly. *We can't kill him, and if we leave him alive, then he'll just kill himself and return in some other form that we don't know about.*

Pixel has a plan, Score answered. *He's just kind of tired right now. We need to borrow some energy from you.* He grinned. *And Marmanki, since he's a magician, but I don't think we'll ask permission first.*

To do what? asked Helaine. She was confident that if Pixel had come up with an idea, it would work. It was astonishing her how much she relied on her friends now.

Transport us all back where we came from — the three of us and Marmanki.

The false unicorn was growing restless, pawing at the ground uncertainly. *I assume the three of you are planning some kind of trick,* he said suspiciously. *But you must know it won't work. I can't be beaten.*

"Talk about overconfidence!" Score said aloud. "Well, we've got news for you. You couldn't be more wrong." He nodded to Helaine. *Follow our lead,* he informed her.

Helaine nodded, and she felt the power build up to a spell forming. It was the transportation spell that the boys had used earlier. *Ambrose ronica presant.* She spoke the words in her mind along with Score and a very faint Pixel, and let their vision of their destination take shape in her thoughts.

Marmanki gave a snort of surprise and alarm, and tried to back away. But it was too late. The web of the spell had tightened about him. As Score had hoped, his own magical ability was helping it to form and be effective.

Then the world reeled for a second, and Helaine felt the strength drain out of her. She almost collapsed from the loss. Now she knew what had happened to Pixel. Teleportation really drained your strength!

She found herself standing inside a vast cavern of snow and ice. Thunder and Nova were waiting impatiently, their breaths clouds of steam in the icy air. Marmanki whuffed in shock, and glared around.

A smart trick, he said, *but it won't help you very much. That transfer drained some of my strength, but I am still in charge here.*

No longer, Thunder replied. *The last time you

faced me, I lost because of your trickery. This time, there will be no tricks. And I shall regain my herd from you.*

Marmanki sneered. *I need no tricks to defeat you, old man!* he cried. *So be it! To the death!* And he lowered his horn and charged at Thunder.

Helaine was still too weak from the transfer to do anything but cry out in shock. Thunder was playing right into Marmanki's hands! He *wanted* to lose this battle and his life.

Then he could take over someone else's body again . . .

CHAPTER 12

Pixel was finally recovering from the energy drain of the teleportation. It hadn't been quite as bad these last two times as it had been the first time he and Score had done it. The reason was obvious — the first time, he and Score had also transported two large unicorns, which took a lot of energy. The second time, when they alone had jumped back to Helaine, had taken less. And this last time, they had drawn on Helaine and Marmanki, too, which made it easier. That meant, if he was correct, that he could probably teleport himself from time to time without getting *too* weak. It was taking along nonmagicians that really drained him.

Still, there was time to think about that later. Right now, the fight was the most important thing. He, Score, Thunder, and Nova had agreed to the plan he had devised, and now Thunder seemed to have thrown it all away because of his wounded pride. He wanted to beat Marmanki in a fair fight.

And it wouldn't *be* a fair fight. Marmanki was provoking Thunder into the battle because he wanted to be killed. He was only going to fake a fight, and then force Thunder into killing him.

Pixel tried to yell all of this out, but he was still too weak. All he could do was to stand there, swaying, and watching the battle.

Marmanki's first charge had been real enough: he had to get Thunder so worked up that Thunder wouldn't think twice about seriously fighting back. Thunder had parried the charge, and then waited for Marmanki to turn and come at him again. It wasn't easy for either unicorn, because underfoot was ice and snow. Somehow, though, their cloven hooves managed to keep their traction on the slippery surface. As Marmanki charged again, Thunder leaped into action.

No! Pixel wanted to yell, but he couldn't. He could see the same panic-stricken looks on the faces of Helaine and Score. They were too tired to call out, either.

At the last second, Marmanki moved his head

aside, baring his throat for a killing thrust from Thunder's horn. Pixel was almost too tense to keep watching, knowing that they had now lost, and Marmanki would be free to take possession of a fresh body.

But Thunder's horn, too, moved aside. Instead of the killing stroke, he left a long furrow of blood down Marmanki's flank. The false unicorn gave an intense scream of pain.

Did you think I would be foolish enough to kill you? Thunder snorted, coming to a halt and turning to face Marmanki once again. *I know your power. You will *not* die through me. But, I promise you, you *will* suffer for what you have done!* And then he charged again.

He does know what he's doing, Pixel realized. He hadn't allowed his emotions to get the better of him. And now Marmanki had no option but to truly fight — not for his life, because that was safe, but to avoid painful injuries that would cripple him and leave him in agony and helpless.

The two unicorns clashed, and fell back. Thunder reared up, striking out with his hooves at Marmanki, who tried to counter. One blow broke open a gash on his forehead though, and made him scream again.

You will lose this fight, blow by blow, Thunder promised him. *But you will not die. You will *suffer.**

Desperately, Marmanki fought back. But this

time he could use no trickery to defeat Thunder. And Thunder was in great form, fighting for his herd and for his own pride. Blow by blow, the fake unicorn was losing the fight.

Pixel finally managed to find his voice. He could feel his strength returning. "Helaine," he gasped. "The agate."

She understood, and managed on the second attempt to clasp hold of the gem, connecting the three of them together mentally. *What is it?* she asked. *Score said that you had a plan.*

I do, he answered. *Thunder's buying us the time we need to get our strength back. You see that large shape in the ice over there?*

Yes, she agreed.

We must free it from the ice, Pixel told her. *That will mean using all of our strength together. None of us has the strength to do it alone at the moment.*

Understood, she agreed. *I'm probably the strongest of us right now, so I'll lead the focus. The two of you follow along.*

Good girl, he said approvingly, and then lent her what little strength he had. For some reason, Score was hanging back, and not contributing. Maybe he was more tired now than Pixel, and it wasn't worth the energy to try and find out.

Together, Pixel and Helaine focused on melting the ice. Reciting the fire spell — *Kula Shriker prior* — she threw a weak fireball at the frozen shape. Pixel was dimly aware of the continuing battle, but he couldn't watch it and concentrate at the same time. Finally, with one last burst of power, the ice had thinned enough for the trapped creature to break free.

It was the ice dragon, of course. Being entombed in ice hadn't hurt it at all, but it had certainly made the creature mad. It looked around for the closest target.

Which was the battling unicorns. Pixel saw that Marmanki had several gashes in his crimson hide now, and that Thunder was untouched. Thunder pressed hard at Marmanki, who was forced to retreat.

Directly into the path of the freed dragon.

Thunder whirled and ran for cover.

Marmanki was suddenly aware of the other creature behind him. He turned to see what was happening, just as a frozen blast from the dragon caught him in its clutches. He froze instantly into a block of ice.

But the dragon was free again, and still mad. It slinked across the floor, looking for other targets. Pixel swallowed. He was still too tired to run, and both he and Helaine were in the open now. The dragon moved slowly toward them, anticipation gleaming in its cold eyes. Pixel whimpered slightly, and tried to drag his exhausted body into motion. But it was no use. He'd used up all of his strength. Even to save his life, he couldn't move.

The dragon sensed this, and reared slowly up to vent its icy breath again.

And the whole roof seemed to collapse onto it in a torrent of water. The deluge froze about it, trapping it once more into an icy clutch.

"Boy," Score gasped, clutching his chrysolite tightly, as if that was all that was holding him upright, "that thing never learns, does it?"

And now Pixel understood why Score hadn't helped them free it. He'd been saving his own energy so that he could make the dragon a captive again when its job was done. "Way to go," he said, approvingly. "I didn't think about getting it back again, did I?"

"You can't think of everything," Score answered with a tired but cheery grin. "I just backed up your plan this time."

"And very well, too," Helaine said. She looked at the block of ice holding Marmanki. "A terrific solution. He's trapped inside there, neither alive nor dead. So he's completely helpless. Until spring."

"Relax," Pixel assured her. "The dragon keeps this place magically chilled forever. And it's now trapped, too. So neither of them will be going anywhere, ever."

A tidy solution, said Thunder. He and Nova had emerged to join the humans. *And I have defeated him to regain my herd. Now there is only one thing that I wish to do.*

"What's that?" asked Pixel.

Get out of this place before my hooves freeze off, he grumbled.

"I second that," Score agreed.

None of you has enough strength to walk, Nova said with sympathy. *So you had better ride us out.*

Marvelous, said Thunder sarcastically. *I'm the leader of the herd again, and what's my first deed? Acting like a _horse_ for human beings.* He glared down at Score and Helaine. *Well, the two of you had better get on before I come to my senses. I hope you at least have the strength for that?*

Pixel managed to clamber onto Nova's back, and saw that Score and Helaine managed to do the same with Thunder. He felt a momentary twinge of jealousy as Score put his arm around Helaine to stay in place. Then, ashamed, he dismissed it. Score wasn't interested in Helaine. It was just for balance.

Hold on! Nova said. *I'm heading back to the warmth as fast as I can!*

EPILOGUE

A week later, they were all feeling a lot better. With Marmanki gone, the spells he had cast on the unsuspecting herd had been mostly removed. Their memories had returned, and they had pledged their loyalty to Thunder once more. Score felt pretty good as he watched the unicorns playing and socializing again.

"They're their old selves again," Helaine said happily. "It's so good to see."

Thanks to the three of you, Flame replied, nuzzling her. *And my father is happier, too. He has his memories of Darkstar back, and at last knows what happened to his friend.*

Score snorted. "Is this where we all start saying *All's well that ends well*?" he asked sarcastically.

"Well, it has," Pixel answered, not rising to the bait. "What's with you? Getting itchy feet or something?"

"Something," Score admitted. "I feel horribly lazy just hanging out here and doing nothing. If you remember, a while back I suggested that we should start to fix the castle up for ourselves as a home."

"You looking for work?" asked Helaine, raising her eyebrows. "This I can't believe. Maybe Marmanki managed to possess you somehow. It doesn't sound like the Score we know talking." She and Pixel were grinning at this, and Score could hear a mental snicker from Flame.

"What I was thinking," he said, refusing to be offended by their humor, "is that this would be a perfect time to go hunting for bicycles and stuff for the castle."

"What's a bicycle?" asked Helaine.

Score grinned nastily. "Something I'm really looking forward to seeing you try and ride," he told her. "What I'm suggesting is that we take a trip to Earth. New York City, to be specific, and pick up some stuff to bring back with us."

"New York?" asked Pixel, brightening up. "That's

the place you're always talking about with the heavenly food?"

"The same," agreed Score. "You guys will *love* the place, I know it."

It sounds like fun, agreed Flame. *I can't wait.*

"What?" Score stared at her, aghast. "No offense, Flame, but New York's not ready for unicorns yet."

*But I *want* to go!*

"No way!" Score was absolutely adamant. "There aren't any unicorns on Earth. You'd just be put into a circus or something. You can't go, and that's definite."

Score gave a sudden cry of pain, and his face turned ashen. He fell to his knees, and then collapsed the rest of the way to the floor. Helaine sprang forward at the same instant Pixel did, and they barely avoided cracking their heads together.

"He's unconscious," Helaine said, worry in her voice. "What happened to him?"

"I can answer that," came Oracle's voice from behind them. "But you aren't going to like it."

Pixel glanced around. He was extremely worried about his friend. "What is it?" he demanded.

"Someone on Earth has placed a spell on him," Oracle answered. "They have his amulet." He, too, looked very concerned. "You'll have to go to Earth to stop this. Otherwise . . ." He stared down at the unconscious Score, and shook his head. "Otherwise, the spell will kill him."

In New York City, the fortune teller straightened up from his crystal ball. "They are coming," he said. His face was lined and tired, and he sat with a stoop. "I cannot be more specific. You and your men will be ready for them?"

"Yes," the hawk-faced man answered. "I'm not sure I believe all this mystic mumbo-jumbo of yours, but you're paying well."

"Very well," agreed the mystic. "You have certain . . . recommendations for being able to do the job I require. You will be able to capture these three children when they arrive?"

"No problem," his companion answered. "You see, I've a . . . *score* to settle with one of them myself." His eyes flashed in anger. "Nobody crosses Bad Tony Caruso without paying for it."

The mystic inclined his head slightly. "One of them has done you an injury?"

"One of them," Bad Tony said coldly, "is my son."